PRAISE FOR MATT BRANDENBURG

"Very funny. Very harrowing. Full of gnarly action. Hell yeah!"

DANGER SLATER, *STARLET*

"A relentless, gory riot! This horror-comedy finds the heart in retribution and a satisfying amount of hilarious mayhem. You'll never look at chocolate the same!"

KIRSTEN NOELLE CRAIG, *THE CURSE OF MEDUA*

"The Dogmen Fudge Incident is insane in all of the best ways: an all gas, no brakes cryptid revenge romp. Read with chocolate."

RYAN C. BRADLEY, *SAY UNCLE*

THE DOGMEN FUDGE INCIDENT

MATT BRANDENBURG

Sleight of Hand Publishing

For my Family

EVEN THOUGH JENN MCKAY had just discovered her husband of over twenty years didn't know how to make a s'more, one of *the easiest* things in the world to make, the day couldn't have been better. The forest near Michigan's pinkie could have been the basis for any number of those cartoon princess fairy tales. Birch, pine, and oak trees with autumn-tipped branches reached up to picture perfect blue skies. A Lake Michigan breeze plucked at golden leaves and made them dance through the trees. An idealized campfire begging to have sticks with marshmallows over it completed the image. Yes, it was almost the best day of all time.

Only problem was the lack of animal sounds.

Plus, the s'more discovery.

The chitter of squirrels, the whistling song of birds, the deep croaking of frogs—all missing from this painting of woodland life. For some people, this would be okay. Who wants to be interrupted from a s'mores lecture by the annoying caw of a crow? Who wants to listen to the chatter of squirrels ridiculing your intelligence?

Winston McKay didn't mind the absent noise. It allowed him to give his full attention to Jenn's throaty gleeful laughter. She might have been mocking him for never making the camping staple, how it was literally only a couple of steps and even a child could do it, but he'd gladly listen to her laugh at his idiocy.

"We've been married how long, and I didn't know this about you? God, it might make me question all my life choices." Jenn scratched her chin, her sparkling violet eyes aimed at the sky pretending to search for an answer, a smile on her face. "I mean, seriously, I've seen you take apart a dryer and put it back together."

"Hey, I'm not a candy maker. All that cooking science stuff, leave it to Alton Brown or what's his name, the cake manager or whoever." Winston stared at the bag of chocolate bars and graham crackers as if they were the ingredients to curing cancer. "Besides, messing with melted chocolate is just gross, who wants that stuff all over their fingers? It's like baby shit."

"Isn't baby shit usually green?"

"Not all the time. It can be all sorts of colors." He shook his head. "Now who doesn't know about things?"

Jenn laughed again, hugged Winston, kissed him hard on the lips. Her mane of silver hair blocking out the world around them. "You are so cute, you silly old man."

"I'm not that old."

"Good, because I've got so much more for us to do!"

Heat flushed Winston's scruffy cheeks as he stared into her wild mischievous face. She had a way about her that made him feel like a teenager again. If it wasn't for Jenn, he probably would have been one of those guys who never left Lansing, never saw the world, never tried sushi, never experienced a downpour on Mount Rainier, never hunted mushrooms in the woods, never learned about s'mores. He'd follow her anywhere, try anything, even deal with melted chocolate on his fingers.

Outside of their conversation, their little circle of love, the quiet forest held its breath. Amongst its trees, a human-sized mass of wrinkly flesh padded to the clearing. Its fur bristled, drool slicking its droopy black lips. It hunched its bulging shoulders and lowered its head attempting to hide behind the baby branches and svelte trees. The creature waited in the shadows, lifting a floppy ear to its prey.

"Another surprise adventure?" Winston said.

Jenn booped him on the nose. "Of course. What's the point in listening to a man-made calendar or worrying about the weather when you could just have fun?"

"I know, I know," Winston said. She always told him they were free to do what they wanted, including the decision to follow her advice. The only thing she wanted him to do was be as free as she felt. But he adored her and never questioned following her on her adventures. "The bills, my doctor, my indigestion might say otherwise, but when did we let them control us, right?"

"Exactly." She floated to the fire, picked up a metal poker, and held a marshmallow to the spike like she was going to give it one more time to fess up on the money it owed. "First, though, I'm going to give you a clinic on s'more making…"

The very simple directions were given in a manner that could be considered "speaking down" or "explaining to a five-year-old" yet Winston still had to concentrate to understand.

Beyond the campfire, and earshot of the two lovers, leaves crunched from the tree line. A low growl rumbled. The swish of a bushy tail wagged at the prospect of an unsuspecting meal.

The beast exploded from the forest on two paws. It howled a deep guess-what-suckas-I'm-here kinda flex. Floppy ears trailed behind its wrinkly head. Jowls rippled and revealed pointy yellowish teeth. Its usually worrisome eyes were now quite excited—all pupils and no whites as it zeroed in on its prey.

Winston and Jenn only had moments to put together what was happening. The s'more would have been perfect, the right amount of brown on the marshmallow, the chocolate soft but not liquid, the graham crackers crisp and sturdy enough to handle the sugar overload. They forgot the snack and spoke in unison, "What the fu—"

The monster slammed into Winston. Claws dug into his shoulders. The oak's bark dug into his back. His shoes dug into the dirt. Jenn let out a manic, murderous scream. He clamped his hands onto the beast's muscly arms thinking he could break free, yet the creature was locked and jacked, and Winston was not.

He hung there against the tree without any idea of what was attacking him. *Is it some sort of mutated dog? Is it a dude in a weird werewolf costume? Did Jenn dope me with some mushrooms?* The questions didn't really matter. All he could focus on was its rotten meat breath misting his face.

Winston wiggled and squirmed, punched and pinched to no effect. Though he did piss it off. With one quick motion it brought its left foot down on Winston's left thigh. Something snapped, dark blood soaked his jeans, and he lost feeling in his leg.

A guttural battle cry stopped the monster. Jenn charged at them, a s'more poker in her hand. Her hair streamed behind her head, her glare at the beast could have withered a lesser creature, her lips curled in a snarl. The air whistled with the swing of her arm. She cracked the bastard right across the back. She lifted her weapon for another attack.

"Yeah, you piece of shit, I'm going to send you back to whatever backyard you came from." Jenn brandished the poker with skill. "I'm going to jab this fucking poker right up your ugly ass nose. Don't you mess with my husband and think you can get away with it."

The half-dog thing craned its neck, snapped its jaws, and barked what Winston could only assume was an oh-hell-no-you-didn't. It let go of him. He winced when his left leg hit the ground and he reached out to the first thing to help his balance. Only problem was that thing was the monster.

As soon as his hand touched its furry back, it lashed out. One of its claws caught him in his left eye. His vision went wobbly before half of his sight blacked out. Liquid from the popped eye streamed down his cheek. The world tilted. His brain fogged over. Somewhere he heard a yelp, a growl, pounding of hairy feet growing distant, Jenn grunting. Pain alarms blared and took over his senses and an internal voice blurted something like, *"We're going down."*

Next thing he knew, trees were sideways, the sky was at his feet, and rocks and twigs dug into his back. Laying in front of him on the ground, or the wall, was Jenn. Blood leaked out of her mouth; bits of her face hung in shreds of flesh. She still held the poker; a chunk of fur clung to the melted chocolate on the metal. He searched for the monster, but it was gone.

"Jenn?"

Nothing. Her eyes didn't hold the same sparkle they used to. Her chest didn't move.

He felt tears slipping down his cheeks, the blood and goo from his missing eye drying on his scruffy face. The trees faded away, the campfire flickered, the sweetness of melted chocolate disappeared. His world went black.

CHAPTER
TWO

A THIN STREAM of steaming hot chocolate sliced through the air and splattered against the target, missing the outline of a half-man half-dog by a mile. The loose brown liquid added another stain to the paper as it traced a line down to the growing puddle on the Formica tile floor. Winston eyed the failure with his one remaining eye as he hissed. He set the red-and-blue striped nozzle down on the cluttered workbench. *Is it the gun, my special mixture, or did I screw up the temperature?* He rubbed the black patch covering his left eye socket. *No, it's the cheap bullshit plastic gun.* No way would it be his chocolate formula or his modifications to the squirt gun, that shit was locked up. Besides, did it really matter? It'd been ten years since his wife made a choice to fight instead of run, ten years since the son of a bitch plucked his eye out and left him with a limp, ten years of trying to live up to what Jenn did and turning up empty handed.

After a minute of running through the mental checklist of fixes and knowing they all sucked, he kicked the neon yellow canister leaning against the table. It was time to get ready for his yearly disappointment. He twisted to crack his spine, observing the culmination of his *golden* years spent in the cramped workspace at the back of his shop.

If you were a child, you'd believe Winston had raided the squirt gun aisle of a toy store and was mad-sciencing the ultimate weapon for a summer of blasting annoying neighbors and whiny friends to hell. Wood benches held disassembled power washers, hand mixers, portable gas grill parts, and even part of a leaf blower. Neon green and orange canisters were streaked with brown. Tubes stuck into hollow fire extinguishers and ended in nozzles, pipes, and lawn sprinklers. Bowls of bubbling chocolate sat above small open flames. Targets, sketches of canine beasts on two legs, and printouts of online articles hung on pegboard walls. Burnt chocolate, sweat, and fart stunk up the air, creating a cloud that'd send anyone with a sense of smell or decency running away. Once upon a time he'd worried the stench would waft into his fudge shop and scare away customers, or Lydia. He stopped caring when he reminded himself the store was supposed to smell like baby poo, that's what people expect when it comes to chocolate. It wasn't the point of why he was here or why he opened the shop.

Winston was shuffling shuffled past the deadly toy arsenal toward the metal door when he caught a flash in the shadows collecting under the staircase. For a split second he was back at the campfire staring into the wrinkly beast's black eyes, claws digging in his skin, nasty meat breath assaulting his nose. His heart punched the inside of his old-man ribs, his killer-trained muscles thrummed for action. A snarl ripped through his lips, his knuckles tightened and begged to beat on something more than tree trunks. If the bastard had finally found him and wanted to finish him off, Winston was only too happy to dare him to try.

The pathetic bell clanking above the shop's front door snapped Winston back to reality. Light flashed off a pair of screws holding a showerhead to a remote-control car he'd given up on and stuck under the staircase.

Adrenaline flushed out of his system and left him deflated. The creak of his bones, the throb of the ancient wound running down his left leg, the phantom reminder of his missing eye combined into a depressing stew bubbling within him. Why couldn't he do the one damn thing he promised his dead wife every year, even if she never asked him.

A tear slipped out of his good eye and found a path down the wrinkles on his gruff face. "Ah shit, you fucking old man, what are you doing?"

Through the watery prism of his vision, he saw his wife's picture tacked to the wall, her mischievous face surrounded by that wild mane of silver hair as she maneuvered over the boulders at the edge of Leelanau Peninsula. She stared at Winston, his past version holding the camera, his future version amongst a pile of hacked Super Soakers.

Failing me is what you're doing. Letting me die over and over. Letting that damn dogman live. Her voice had changed over the years, resembling his own timbre more and more. Winston crumpled inward and wept. Recomposing himself, he puffed up his chest, wiped the snot from his face, punched a two-by-eight covered in duct tape, and steeled himself for going to the memorial.

She had to listen to what he had to say.

Closing the door and triple checking the lock, he entered the sterile kitchen of his fudge shop. As much as he preferred the cramped workshop's clutter, he took pride in the stainless-steel tables, broiler, knives, cold blocks of granite, and wall of refrigerators that made up the kitchen. It's here he cooked up the fudge, taffy, caramel things, mint chocolate stuff, other cocoa-based products you'd assume would be in a fudge shop, including chocolate cheese (look it up). The more important part, however, was the chocolate ammunition for the guns, which he usually made after hours or while bored and ignoring customers, which ended up being most of the time and most of the shop's stock.

On a rolling table near the front of the store lay a bouquet of daisies, his wife's favorites. She would have laughed thinking about him in this fancy kitchen, making chocolate treats.

"...then they found out the class was completely fake! It was some crazy ploy to get them all to buy suitcases, for some random reason." Lydia Evan's raspy voice filled the empty store. She tilted her head, spiky raven black hair vibrating at the movement, at the clop of Winston's boots as he entered the customer area. Fluorescent lights flashed across her glasses.

"What are you doing here?" Winston said. Lydia pointed at herself and then toward a lanky man in a brown plaid shirt and khakis, his brown limp hair combed to the side of a bland face with chunky brown glasses.

The man pointed his thumb to a brown Ford F150 parked out front. "I thought you wanted me to pick you up now."

"Not you, Bill. Her."

Lydia cocked an eyebrow and glanced around as if searching for an audience. "Last I checked, we were open today. You didn't hear me come in an hour ago?"

It'd been about a year since he hired her. She helped with customers and ran the shop a lot more than he expected, even if she constantly jabbered at him. Somehow, she never took the hint when he grumbled or delivered a smartass comment about the joys of silence.

Winston swore he told her they'd be closed today. Or at least put it on a calendar. He knew he at least *thought* about telling her. "Well, we're not. So, I guess you can leave, after you clean and close the place up."

"A thanks for coming in or a gee, enjoy a day off, would be nice," Lydia whispered.

Winston glared at her with his one eye. He and his wife never had kids, yet somehow, he had picked up the skill of conveying disappointment with a single look. Her face flushed and she reached under the counter for the cleaning supplies.

"Come on, man, go easy on her. She's just doing her job." Bill's voice reminded Winston of beige. "If you don't treat her right, I'll hire her at my store."

Gritting his teeth, Winston turned his gaze onto Bill. If he didn't need the man to drive him to the south side of town, he would've booted him into the October chill. They might hang out in the alley behind their shops, smoking the occasional cigarette and bad-mouthing North Leeland, but Winston didn't want to see the guy as anything more than a neighbor. "Do you really need someone to help sell all that goofy shit? How many people are buying those fake bargain paintings?"

Bill snorted, squirting mucus out of his nose. His face reddened and he wiped at the snot with a brown paisley hand-kerchief, leaving a bit of green goo on his upper lip. As he stuffed the wet square of fabric in his pocket, he shook his head. "Welp, you ready to go?"

Winston held up the daisies as if they were going to ward off the man going out of his way to help him. His blood ticked up a few degrees and he cursed the monster for putting him in the position of needing others. Knowing he had to sit in a truck with the guy, he directed his super positive energy to Lydia. "Make sure to clean the space between the counters and the gunk around the refrigerators. There was some gross shit there the other day and I don't need the health inspector on my ass."

Lydia faked gagging. "There's really nothing worse than melted chocolate shit in a fudge shop."

She saluted Winston as the two men left her alone.

Winston stared out the truck's window, ignoring Bill as they drove down Pine Street. For the thousandth time he questioned his decision to open the fudge shop in the most northern building in town while his wife's memorial was on the southern outskirts. If he had been smart, they would have been located within walking distance of each other, and he wouldn't have to sit here listening to Bill's piss-poor attempt at conversation.

As they passed another tacky tourist shop, he pushed away his doubts. North Leeland sat on the coast of Lake Michigan at the base of Michigan's pinkie. Pine Street cut through town and was the only street in and out of the geological little finger. Tourists were forced through Winston's burg on their way to get drunk in the woods, drown in the water, collect mosquito bites, and basically be a pain in his ass during the summer months. He'd assumed most of them would be so hopped up on summertime fun they'd ignore his shop on the drive. As for Jenn's memorial bench, well, the town was her favorite town in the state. She thought the forest south of North Leeland was the most magical area in the country. It only made sense to put the memorial bench close to the town and woods she died in.

When they reached the town square, Bill brought up—for the millionth time—how empty the town seemed. Did the man forget this was the same every year near the end of October? Winston appreciated this season, with its calm, the lack of obnoxious people stopping into this shop, and the quiet preceding the town's upcoming hibernation. He did his best to forget the Chamber of Commerce's attempt at attracting people with their dumb pig roast today. Even if the charred meat aroma made his mouth water. Citizens took their time strolling down the street, and the owner of a competing fudge shop adjusted their Halloween decorations. If North Leeland could always be this barren, and he could focus on hunting the monsters down, he'd probably be in a much better mood.

"Aww jeez, I hate to do this to you, but I gotta stop for gas real quick." Bill's voice cut through Winston's thoughts. He grunted a response as they pulled into the Wesco gas station.

A few trucks and cars were in front of the station or at pumps, the drivers staring at the video screens advertising cheap hot dogs, or near the entrance smoking and checking out the other customers. Everyone glanced at the sky as the monthly tornado siren test cried out its haunting drone. Winston weighed going in for a coffee or stewing in the truck. The last thing he wanted to do was deal with random townsfolk, but sitting here while Bill droned on through the window seemed worse. Without a glance at his driver, he limped to the gas station. He itched his eye patch, set his face to grimace mode, and focused on getting in and out.

Wesco was your typical gas station: aisles of snacks, a wall of coolers full of drinks and worms for bait, a coffee area, and a few spinners with nasty-looking hot dogs. Winston thought about checking to see if they were selling any of his fudge, Lydia was in charge of getting their product in places like this, but he didn't care to look. Besides, he saw the group of men in their neon orange camouflage and idiotic trucker hats advertising John Deere and a cooler company, for some reason. They were discussing the annual pig roast and how much they were going to stuff their maws with burnt meat. The conversation died as he stifled a groan and shuffled to the coffee.

"Oh hey, you guys see any of those killer dogs out there?" The hint of a drawl dragged the question over Winston's shoulder. He grabbed a Styrofoam cup.

The group's laughter echoed through the store. Someone slapped the back of another. "I heard they sorta look like bears."

"And they're attracted to the smell of meth."

More guffaws and back slapping. One even snorted. Winston filled his cup with black coffee. His hand didn't shake, and he didn't glance at the idiots. They couldn't even come up with something new. Why did everyone in town say the exact same thing? They could at least have a meeting to create new theories.

"You know, for some strange reason, we are always running out of squirt guns. And what's weird is that Bobby keeps telling me some old man is buying them." This voice Winston recognized. Carl over at the Toy Castle. A drunk that overcharged for cheap plastic. If Winston cared, he'd turn around and tell the bastard that his store sucked, but the toy store owner meant less than shit to him.

"It does make you wonder if he's trying to trick kids into his place. Man owns a candy store and has toys? Something ain't right with him."

Winston swallowed the hate building in his throat. Everyone in town sucked. They were worthless and he wished they'd all accidentally shoot themselves while hunting. Why did that fucking dogman have to kill Jenn here? Why did he dedicate himself to the monster's eradication? And why the hell couldn't he find where they were hiding? He left the gas station and its hateful laughter. Bill sat in the truck, smiling his bland smile. The two continued their trek without a word, Winston sipping on burnt coffee, Bill gabbing about the weather.

The town thinned into starter homes overlooking the coast before hitting North Leeland's edge. Dirt patches and parking spots allowed people to pull over and get pictures of the beautiful blue water. On the road's left side stood the primordial forest. It'd been ten years since his wife's murder, ten years of building kooky weapons and halfassing his way through business ownership and he still hadn't been able to find the fucking monster that ruined his life.

He saw the lonely bench facing the water before Bill spoke. "Ope, looks like we're here."

Winston cleared his throat, a mixture of shame, annoyance, and appreciation clogging up his chest. "I...I want to thank you for doing this. If it wasn't for this damn limp and eye. Dammit, it'd have taken me all day."

"Hey, man, don't mention it." He pulled the Ford over. "I'll be here whenever you're ready."

The wood and metal bench offered a picturesque view of the uninterrupted lake. White caps decorated the surface. A few crows cawed. Browning leaves whispered secrets about the beast lurking under their canopy. Winston focused on the emptiness of the Great Lake. When he reached the bench, he traced a finger on the plaque attached to the top plank.

Jennifer McKay

Brightening the day of all she met. Please enjoy this moment of nature and peace.

Staring out at the water, he let his mind float.

"Jenn, ten long friggin' years. It's been so goddamn hard without you. Sorry for the cussing, by the way, but you know me and how I get sometimes. I'm trying to be good; I promise. And I've been—"

Behind him, a truck door creaked open. He grunted, assuming Bill went to piss in some trees.

"I've looked almost everywhere. All my focus is on hunting them down. You should see the shop, so many ways to kill them. With the girl there, I have so much more time now. But you probably know that. I assume as a ghost or whatever, you probably see it all. Which means you're probably aware every year I check our spot; I come up empty handed.

"I just don't think I can face finding nothing anymore. I know I said last year that I would, but…"

The eyepatch strap itched the side of his head. Tears slipped down his cheek. He slammed a fist against his thigh and told himself to stop being a fucking coward.

"Remember how I swore I could fix the dryer? How many times did I screw it up worse? But I got it to work, eventually. It's one of the things you said you loved about me. That no matter how much of a failure I felt like, I didn't stop.

"Well, I think this is one time I'm going to stop. And I'm sure you're happy about that. I know you wanted me to be free, but I couldn't sit by and let that bastard live. Not after it took away one of the best people ever. I had to try, and now I feel like I'm failing…"

He held his head, hoping Bill wouldn't see him sobbing.

"I love you and think about you all day. I'm just so tired."

An earth-cracking howl rattled his bones. Goosebumps

pimpled his skin. The deep wound in his leg throbbed. Winston winced and faced the truck. Bill was nowhere in sight.

"Uh, hey Bill, where you at?" Part of him hoped he'd made up the sound, that Bill was passed out in the truck. The other part prayed it was something much worse. "I'll see you, Jenn."

Halfway to Bill's truck, he saw his neighbor booking it out of the woods, his bland face now a shade of white, his mouth contorted into a grimace, his eyes wild. He finally looked interesting.

"We gotta get the fuck out of here!"

LYDIA STEPPED out of Winston's Fudge Shop into an overwhelming aroma of cooking meat that almost made her stop wondering what the hell was going on with her boss. He'd been hiding all morning in his *secret* workroom grumbling, cracking something plastic, and cooking up some awful burnt chocolate stank. She even heard a hiss and splatter she swore was the same noise a Super Soaker made as it blasted a kid in the face. Then, there was that whole not realizing she was there. The dude was losing his mind.

No one else in town was hiring when she found The Fudge Shop. Her stomach always turned when Jeff or her mom suggested finding a new job. Why would she want to go through the hunt again or deal with getting used to a new place? It was easier to just put up with Winston and the customers. A year of dealing with the guy and his antics, nothing was shocking. At least the hours weren't terrible, and it was a paycheck. How she got paid she had no idea; the place was never busy. Her only guess was he had squirreled away money.

Besides, her bitterness should be directed at her friends meeting without her at Left Coast Coffee Works. They knew she had to work all day, yet Jeff still suggested they hold a study session. Troy and Gillian even agreed to the time. She understood why. They had midterms and exams coming up, while she had nothing happening in the next couple of weeks except for stocking peppermint fudge. And while she would never want them to fail and have to stay in town with her longer, it still hurt that they were pulling away. Besides, they probably weren't even really studying. Lydia knew most of the time they were just slacking off. Why couldn't they have waited until she had a day off? Jerks.

"Ah man, don't tell me you're not open?" The nasally voice creeped over her back. "I was really hoping to get a bar of fudge."

Lydia scrunched up her face, sagged her shoulders, and turned. He stood a little too close and breathed through his mouth, the top of his pale shaved head almost level with the top of the shop's door. The edges of his chapped lips curled in what she thought might be a smile but looked more like an impression of a duck. The man wore baggy ill-fitting jeans and an orange zip-up jacket. She reached for the keys, then stopped, an image of her friends finishing early and leaving before she got a chance to see them popped into her head. Her chest hollowed and her thoughts bounced back and forth on what to do. *Winston would probably be cool with me turning this down.* "Yeah, sorry. We're closed for the day. Maybe come back tomorrow?"

"I really like your hair."

"Wait, what?"

They never got much foot traffic this far from the center of town and she wondered if the stores across the street had any customers looking out the windows. She guessed they were probably all getting ready for the pig roast. Lydia snuck a hand into her bag, searching for her phone or Bluetooth speaker to smack upside this guy's skull. He was all skin and bones. One hit would take him out.

He chuckled, the noise reminding her of squeaky toys and cartoons. "I don't think I'll be able to come back tomorrow."

The man rubbed the side of his shaved head, glanced at his dirty New Balance, then brought his gaze back to her. "Actually, I was wondering, is the owner in? Or maybe you might know, did he really see a monster in the woods?"

Fuck, that's what the dude wants. Winston had warned her about Big Government trying to catch him lying about what had happened to his wife. No one believed it was a half-dog half-man that killed her. Even Lydia didn't buy the story. A man that was a dog? What a crazy idea. His wife probably had a heart attack or something and he came up with the goofy monster angle because he's weird. She humored Winston, only because she didn't want to make him sad. This guy didn't look like he was FBI or CIA, or whoever investigated that kind of stuff. Maybe he was one of those cryptid hunters, podcaster dudes. While she was onboard for the mysterious, she hated how cruel these jerks came off, like they were making fun of Winston. Lydia knew exactly what to do with people like this asshole. "You know, the last guy that asked him this walked away with a broken nose. The guy before that had two black eyes. Maybe you should check the woods yourself? It'd be safer."

He straightened, an ugly smile plastered back on his face. The monthly tornado siren drill cut through his giggling. He coughed, glanced around then laughed again. "And I've been in the woods. It's very nice."

She cocked her head. "Well, alright then. I gotta go."

The dude watched her, his stupid grin unwavering. Lydia shuffled backwards. In the distance, a howl coasted along the air. Along with the haunting tornado alarm, the town seemed to have weird timing for testing their scary sounds CD. It was enough to send her hustling down Pine Street toward the coffee shop. Hopefully her friends were still there, she was ready for them to offset the strange morning.

BILL DIDN'T STOP RUNNING until he slammed into the truck, wheezing. Winston urged his aching leg muscles into action, worried his store neighbor was about to ditch him. *What scary thing did he stumble onto?*

Bill cranked the key, and the Ford jumped to life. He slammed his palm against the steering wheel over and over before Winston could even open the door. He did his best to hobble into the passenger seat.

"What the hell is bothering you?" Winston said.

"Cheese and crackers!" For the first time since Winston met the guy, Bill didn't sound like he was the audio version of a tax form. The truck kicked up a cloud of dust as it fishtailed onto the road. Bill's focus bounced all over the place, always returning to the rearview mirror. "Darn thing came out of nowhere."

"What?"

"I must be crazy, maybe tired. It was probably just a momma bear protecting its cubs."

"A bear?"

Winston craned his neck and stared out the back window. A dark shadow emerged from the woods. It zeroed in on them and chased after the truck. Winston's eye outgrew the oversized cookies he'd baked. "Shit! I think you pissed it off!"

The beast tore at the ground with all four legs, picking up speed, before it rose onto its hindlegs. Winston's heart skipped a beat. *No.* He could make out enough of its vague shape and knew it wasn't a bear. *Could it be?* The creature gained on them.

"You better speed up," Winston said. The outcropping of tall pines marking the boundary between town and nature didn't seem like it was coming up fast enough. The Wesco gas station and Cheeseman's Sandwich Emporium, the eyesore of a metal cell tower peered through the trees, taunting him.

After all these years of nothing, was it really the monster now chasing him? Sweat trickled down his face. The wound on his leg throbbed. His mind replayed the faithful day in the forest, the wrinkly beast with its glistening fangs, the black claw slicing across his face and popping his eye, the way his wife beat on the monster without hesitation, the way it disappeared, leaving Jenn's corpse and Winston's life behind.

All the maps in his workshop showed red x's all over the upper part of the lower peninsula, a big circle over the spot he lost his wife. Ten years of dragging himself back to the scene of the murder, of hunting through every forest and wooded area, and he hadn't found a monster yet. *It can't be possible, it can't be here, not now.*

Sucking in a deep breath, he faced the road behind them again. The shape had gained more ground, giving Winston further clarity on what was chasing them. The floppy ears, the jowls flapping in the wind, the tongue lolling out, the wagging tail. He closed his eye as his whole world dropped out from below him.

A motherfucking dogman was chasing their motherfucking truck.

"Fudge, what the hell is that?" Bill said, panic ratcheting his voice to a manic whine.

Winston whipped around in time to spot the ugly cell tower wobbling. It crumpled into itself before tumbling into the forest. Muscular upright dog human shapes ran and ducked into the copse of trees near the Wesco.

"Holy fuck," Winston said, and cursed himself for not packing more than a single goddamn chocolate bar. He usually never left home without one, he must have been distracted. How could he have forgotten the pocket chocolate bulb, which he'd dubbed "Chocolate Squirts," or the hollow knife full of a concentrated mix of his special formula? Despite not caring what the townsfolk thought, he didn't want to be like that one weird old man in every town, carrying a squirt gun full of chocolate and raving about monsters. Even though this time the fucking thing was real. Anger and frustration replaced the other emotions and became the columns holding up the one thing that'd get him through this.

Vengeance.

Time slowed to a crawl, making him feel each agonizing second the beast chased them. Winston rocked back and forth as if that'd help Bill's truck speed up. Even in the middle of a monster chase, the guy would never break the law and go past the speed limit.

Movement amongst the tree trunks on the right side of the road chilled his blood. A group of dogmen pointed at the road. Further in were more dogmen, bounding and circling the others, tails wagging, jaws snapping, arms pointing, legs lifted moments before peeing. A few monsters congregated near the tall pines, barking back at the ones pointing. Winston squinted. They appeared to be pushing and rubbing against the bottom of the trees. *What the hell are they doing?*

"Oh shit, watch out!"

The thick trees toppled onto the road.

Bill slammed on the brakes. Burning rubber filled the cabin. An awful screech sliced ear drums. Someone squealed. Urine splashed on floorboards. A terrible metallic crunch. Winston's seat belt tightened against his chest. His head flew forward. Glass shattered. Blackness came.

JEFF WAS ALREADY SEATED at the head of the table by the time Lydia made it to Left Coast Coffee. The same spot he always claimed whenever they all hung out. They never really questioned it, they enjoyed sitting next to each other, and with Jeff at the front they could easily listen to him. Troy and Gillian were on the same side, he whispered to her, and she forced out a pity laugh. Jeff smirked as he took a sip from his espresso. He glanced at the door and beamed at Lydia.

He motioned to a chair. "You're here? Didn't expect to see you."

She dropped her bag, the *Aliens* and *Predator* buttons clicking together, and sat down. A few textbooks were on the table, none of them open. "Yeah, Winston closed the shop early. See you're getting a lot of studying done."

"We were going to get started, I swear." Troy opened the cover, the spine cracking like it was brand new. "How'd you get lucky enough to have a free day? And, like, I don't get how that place is still open. I never see any customers."

"I have a strong feeling it's insurance money—plus, he never buys anything. I swear the dude hasn't changed his clothes for the last year. I think all the kitchen stuff was bought used, too.

As for getting out early, I don't know, he had flowers and looked upset."

Troy closed the book and laughed. "That tracks about the money. And maybe he's got a date and knows it's going to end with him getting dumped. Doesn't he always look pissed?"

Gillian shook her head and patted Troy on the arm. "Nice try, but I don't think so. No one's going to date him. He'd probably freak out on them or something."

Flashes of tourist women hitting on him ran through her mind. For being a grumpy old man, he somehow got a lot of attention. Maybe it was the eyepatch? She didn't know, but she couldn't believe how many of them asked to see his taffy puller or how much cream he made. She shuddered at the thought of him in any position like that. After each one, he'd stare at the ceiling, mumble the name Jenn, then stomp off into the back.

"Yeah, I don't think he's really into dating people." Lydia scanned the tables of customers, her focus settling on a woman on her phone ignoring her boy as he stuffed his face with a chocolate muffin. "Anyway, there was this super skeevy dude waiting outside the store when I left."

Troy opened his mouth, a sparkle in his eye, then closed it when Jeff cut him off. "That's weird. I saw a pervy guy at the gas station on the way here. It's just this town, it's full of gross people."

"Maybe the BBQ is attracting all the creeps, or there's some weird dude migration, like ducks, but they go up north instead of south," Troy said.

The group cracked up at Troy's attempt at a joke as Lydia went to order a coffee. When she came back, they settled into their routine of half studying for their Lake Michigan College classes, half talking shit about people. Lydia recognized some of the names mentioned, back when she attended. She nodded along or forced a laugh when everyone else found something funny, otherwise spun the coffee cup around. Jeff did his best to guide the conversation to include her or steer it away from

Gillian and Troy chatting about their weekend plans. The Fudge Shop, Winston, the creepy dude, and the lingering frustration around them planning this hangout while she was working disappeared from Lydia's thoughts. Time slunk to whatever corner it hid in when friends were together, and all was good with the world.

CHAPTER
SIX

WINSTON GROANED and rubbed a sticky spot on the side of his head. A whisper of air tickled his skin. Distant screams and growls floated through the truck's busted windows. He did an internal check, testing his limbs for movement. It all hurt like a son of a bitch. The world appeared liquid and out of focus when he sat up. He blinked until it cleared and noticed the empty seat, the driver-side door hanging on its hinge, the torn stuffing, the drops of red, the brown fabric of khaki pants.

"Bill?" he croaked.

The seat belt dug into his chest, and he winced as he struggled to escape. A few birds sang, Lake Michigan lapped against the shore, the wind whistled through the broken windshield. Steadying himself, Winston limped to Bill's side of the truck. The fallen trees had flattened the front of the F150. Red, yellow, and orange bits of plastic, chunks of metal, and frayed wires were scattered across the concrete. A streak of blood and muddy prints circled the area near the driver-side door.

"Bill!" He lost the croak in his voice.

Rustling leaves in a copse of trees between the road and the lake grabbed his attention. A hairy bulging shape was bent over a shadow of a body, a shaggy part of the shape wagging.

"Shit. Fuck. Shit." Winston squinted at the body on the ground and recognized the twitching boots. *Bill.*

Even though he always gave Bill a hard time, always resented asking for a drive, always grumbled at the man's bland smile, Winston's heart sank at the sight of his sorta friend. He thought about the times they'd commiserate about the town's shitty government, the shared cigarettes and beer, the times Bill listened to him rattle on about monsters.

The jagged shape shuddered; a hairy muscly limb thrashed at Bill's torso. Weak groans mingled with deep snarls. Bits of cloth and blood flew. One of his arms was ripped off with a pop and tossed aside. Bill squeaked out a "fiddlesticks" before a horrible snap and Bill's head rolled down the incline toward the lake.

"Oh my god, no." Winston's mind tried processing the decapitation, and how it wouldn't have happened if Bill hadn't been here. If only he hadn't made his sorta friend come here.

The dogman stood, revealing its muscular ten-foot-tall body. Two floppy ears hung from the spotted wrinkly furry head; its jowls dripping with Bill's blood. It stared at the sky and howled one of those yodel howls some dogs do.

Winston reeled and hobbled back to the truck. He ducked, an awkward pain digging into his thigh. Did the dogman spot him? Why did Bill have to go into those woods? Why did Bill have to be so nice and willing to drive him here every year? He cursed himself for not instantly reacting and attacking, hated that he'd been training for years and when he finally faced one, he did nothing. Yet, he couldn't help himself, he couldn't get up, couldn't stop his body from shaking. Something crinkled. *Get up and fight, old man.* No matter how many times he said it, he couldn't do much more than rub his annoying leg. He felt a rectangular lump. Confused, he dug into his pocket and pulled out a bar of chocolate. He leaned against the truck, squeezed the sugary salvation, and a bit of his strength stirred.

The dogman stalked into view, dwarfing the F150 as it rounded the tailgate. It'd been ten fucking years since he'd last seen one in real life. It had haunted his dreams, hounded his steps, crept through the shadows of his life. This creature looming over the F150 didn't match the one that had killed his wife, that beast was seared in his mind. But it didn't matter to him. Rage burned and bubbled inside him, his body tremored, the chocolate bar squished in his grip, and he felt the first inklings of losing his shit, in a good way.

The monster curled its black lips, a red tongue hid behind dagger-like teeth, and released a torrent of earth-shattering barks. All the vague reports of a dog human creature from drunk rednecks online—shitty sketches he found on goofy message boards—didn't give the beast in front of him enough credit. Seeing a dogman in real life, towering over him, the razor-sharp claws pointing at Winston's throat and glint of murder in its black eyes, was enough to make Winston question ever checking the internet. The dogman's muscles rippled as it tightened to leap, and he forgot all his research.

Normally in these moments, time stops or becomes thick and slow as molasses. Usually there's slow motion and flashes of the past, it takes forever for the participants and action to actually happen. In this case it's definitely not that, no flashy tricks or delays. Maybe it was the years of Winston's pent-up rage, maybe it was piss-inducing fear, maybe it was the real biz and not movie, fiction-writing bullshit. Whatever it was, he had no control over his actions and couldn't stop to think about what he was doing.

With the chocolate bar half-melted in his hand, he leapt at the monster the same moment it did. One old man body and one hairy dog-like body crashed together. Rancid breath washed over Winston's face. The monster snapped at Winston, missing by mere centimeters. With an elbow, he cracked it in the jaw, teeth clicking together. The response was a claw to his arm, ripping a chunky bit from his bicep. He fell back a step, and it pressed its advantage, following and pinning him against the truck with its muscly arms on either side of his body. Winston punched it in the gut and busted his knuckles, the monster staring at him with a is-that-all-you-got look. A twinge of fear flickered in him when it reared back its head, opened its jaws, released its stank-ass breath, tilted its head slightly and went in for the kill.

Moving with a quickness that took years to master, he jammed the chocolate bar deep into the creature's throat. Its jaws snapped shut on his arm before he could release the candy. Pointy teeth punctured tough elderly skin. His fingers popped open, dropping the soft bar onto the tongue. The monster hacked, allowing Winston to yank his hand out. Its eyes bulged and flashed with a crazed expression. Stumbling back, it cocked its head in that adorable way dogs do. The beast hunched its shoulders, bent its neck, its cheeks ballooning out. Winston leapt and clamped both of his hands around the creature's snout. His weight bent the dogman's knees, bringing it down level with him. Brown goo dribbled out the monster's lips as it growled and whined.

"Just swallow it, ya bastard."

The plan was inspired by his mom forcing their family dog to swallow pills. Winston shook the dogman's head, then forced the snout up to the sky. *Shit, how am I going to do this next part?* The pause gave the monster a chance to swipe at his chest. Claws ripped gashes through shirt and skin. It grumbled and pressed up to its full height, giving Winston a target: its hairy neck. Winston growled and headbutted its neck, leaving his forehead against the furry throat. He nodded his head in a yes-you-are-going-to-swallow-this and no-you-won't-spit-it-out gesture. When he felt its Adam's apple bob, he flashed a wicked grin. *Works for dogs and dogmen.*

Its guts grumbled. A horrible stench of chocolate and meat billowed out and misted Winston. He backed away, his face twisted in disgust, his muscles tense. The monster's snout and lips twitched, it belched and panted, and clawed at its throat. Winston pictured percolating chocolate mixing with stomach acids, blood and fluids pumping to fight the toxins. The dogman doubled over holding its stomach. A loud whine whistled through its teeth. Round black eyes rolled back moments before a vile stream of blood and chocolate exploded out of its mouth. Vomit splashed onto the concrete and formed a frothy puddle. Winston gagged from the blend of burnt chocolate and nasty-ass-liquid-shit-in-a-steaming-outhouse stench. The monster fell to its knees before toppling into the goo. More soupy hot chocolate flowed out of its mouth, changing from brown to red as its insides fled the dying body. With one last snort, it stopped moving.

Tears slipped out of Winston's good eye, and he collapsed. His breath heaved and rattled in his lungs. Muscles that'd trained for—but never experienced—a battle with a monster quaked. The cuts on his body stung and oozed. His arm with the chunk missing burned and it hurt any time he attempted to move. He gritted his teeth and ignored the pain while he stared at what had been the sole focus of his last decade, the thing that'd stolen his wife from him. The sickly stink of chocolate, throw-up, and monster excrement clouded the area. The pathetic dogman lay in its own puke and shit.

Winston glanced at the brown and red smeared across his hand. *Glad the chocolate actually worked, otherwise I would have been fucked.* In his darker nights, he worried all of his work was nothing but a distraction. He turned his attention to the blue sky. "Well, Jenn, I guess I'm not done yet. I swear I'll find the one that took you."

A breeze blew in from the water, clearing the air of the awful stank and caressing his cheek. He smiled, wanting to believe this was her smacking him and saying, *My old man. You don't have to swear to me. But you do need to listen.*

When the wind died down, a howl filled the emptiness. Winston's skin prickled, his phantom eye pulsed. *Oh god.*

Tendrils of black smoke rose into the sky above North Leeland. Screams, the squeal of brakes, and a chorus of howls chilled his blood. Vague shapes ran across Pine Street. Menacing shadows bounded after them. Winston exhaled, balled his fists, and set his sights toward town. His shop—his armory of chocolate-filled dogmen-killing weapons—called to him.

A LOUD ANGRY howl busted up the group's fun.

Customers quieted and scanned the street outside through the floor to ceiling windows at the front of the cafe. The howl felt dangerous and not at all what you'd find on a novelty Spooky Sounds CD.

"Jeez, they're really upping their game for next week's Halloween parade." Gillian said.

Jeff leaned back. "I doubt that. They can't even fix the broken sidewalks in front of my place. Or what about the pier? It's practically crumbling, no wonder only the police boat is tied to it."

The howl weaseled its way into Lydia's primal self, warning her a predator was close, and she should hide. Despite the way the others smiled, she noticed the twinge of fear in their eyes, the tension in their bodies.

Troy leaned over the table. "I bet it was a werewolf. It's close to a full moon, we're surrounded by woods, perfect spot for them to hunt."

The rest of them waited for a punchline. When he sunk back into his chair, with his eyebrows scrunched over his eyes, his mouth in a line, they realized it wasn't a joke.

Gillian snorted before laughing. "Are you serious?"

"What? They could be real."

Lydia offered up a sad smirk. "Troy, come on."

Jeff shook his head. "First of all, no, they can't. Second, if we were to think they were real, it's daylight out. And with that, let's wrap this up, I've got things to do."

"Sure you do, like nap and play on your phone," Gillian said. "But, yeah, I need to get ready for—"

A faint tea kettle-like scream invaded the coffee shop. Someone groaned, another person cursed. Troy nodded, pointed at his friends and told them he was right. The cry outside had an edge to it that plucked Lydia's spine. Another howl overpowered the panicked noise. Jeff sighed, sat up, and glared at the wall-sized windows, the others turning to join in on the stare-off with outside. The empty street and the shops on the other side took on the challenge and stared back. The scream reached a knitting-needles-stabbing-your-eardrums level as a woman sprinted into view outside.

Pink lipstick, rose blush, and dark eyeshadow streaked the woman's face. Her leather purse bounced off her hip. She slowed when she reached the door and put a hand on her chest.

Lydia glanced at her friends, wondering who'd get up first to help. Probably Jeff, he always took charge. All they did was stare at the panicked woman. So, fighting the urge to follow their lead and do nothing, she stood. She took only a few steps to help the lady when a shadowy hulking shape bounded in from the left, the coffee shop's window acting like a TV screen playing a horror movie.

The woman yelped. Her hands shook as her slick palm slipped off the door handle. No one inside the coffee shop moved. Lydia wanted to help, wanted to open the door. Her muscles had other plans, like doing nothing. Would the others do something? Jeff had to be jumping up to help, right? Yet everyone was mesmerized by the beast rearing back, revealing its terrible glory.

The only thought in Lydia's mind was: *monsters are real.*

CHAPTER
EIGHT

THE BEAST outside of Left Coast Coffee Works released a throaty bark before focusing on the elderly lady in its grip. Lydia didn't want to believe what she was seeing. Maybe it was a person in a costume? There's no way this existed in the real world. At its full height, the cafe's floor-to-ceiling windows only revealed its muscular shoulders, leaving its head a mystery. Wiry black hair covered its body, with tan and white hairs on its chest and surprisingly-toned stomach. A furry tail stood straight out. Black claws on the end of four fingers promised pain as the creature slashed the woman. Deep cuts ripped through fabric and bicep, sending blood splattering against the door. The beast lowered its head. Pointy ears, golf ball-size black eyes, a snarling muzzle with a wet nose, and glistening drool hanging from black lips completed the nightmarish picture. It clamped onto the woman's neck, turning her scream into a wheezing gasp, and shook her like a chew toy.

"It's a motherfucking werewolf!" Troy said.

While the werewolf tore into the woman, people screamed, covered their faces, cried, and someone amongst the customers pissed themself. One of the beast's silky black ears twitched toward the coffee shop while the rest of its head focused on the human snack. Blood dripped off its snout, mingling with the crimson oozing out of the woman's mouth and splattering against the sidewalk. Her limbs flopped around as if they were rubber. Her head hung at a wacky angle, giving the beast easy access to chew neck tissue.

Lydia's internal system glitched and froze, leaving her stuck watching the massacre without the ability to run or help. *Have I ever seen her before? Did she live in town?* Her brain built an image of grandchildren, of her taking them to Winston's Fudge for candy, of them buying those dusty Warren Inn Creme Eggs and *not* touching the display case with their chocolatey fingers. The vision shattered when the woman's head plopped off her leaving behind a tree stump of flesh geysering blood.

"Lydia, what the fuck? We gotta go." Jeff grabbed her shoulder and spun her away from the carnage. Troy kept babbling about how he knew werewolves existed.

Her functions sputtered back to life, loads of questions blossoming in her head. Only one made it to her mouth. "Is this for real?"

Jeff wrapped her in a hug as he pulled her toward the back of the shop.

"Wait, maybe we can help her?"

"Her head is currently on the sidewalk. So, no. I think we need to worry about us." Jeff rushed her past their table to a spot near the counter. Most of the customers were huddling as far away from the glass wall as possible. Lydia couldn't help herself and glanced back outside. One of the woman's torn arms hung from the door handle, blood trickling out of the jagged limb. The monster flopped down on its back right into the ripped-apart torso and began squirming and rolling around, snorting as it coated itself in her goo. Jeff gathered the group, pulling her gaze away from the horrific sight. "We are going to hide, wait for this—"

"Werewolf," Troy said.

Jeff squinted at Troy. "—murderer to leave. Then high tail it to our cars and get the fuck out."

"We should call the cops first," Lydia said.

"More like animal control." Troy kept watching the monster. "Damn, it's peeing on her body."

"Troy, shut up," Gillian said, pulling out her phone. A red X appeared where it usually showed 5G. "Shit. Anyone else want to call?"

Lydia and Jeff both checked and had similar results.

Jeff stuffed his phone back in his pocket. "Whatever, I'm sure someone's already called—"

The cafe's front window shattered, pieces of glass crashing against the hardwood floor. A musky scent mixed with copper and a hint of BBQed pork wafted into the area and overpowered the coffee aroma. A child screamed, a woman cried out for Jesus, someone yelled fuck over and over. The beast growled before popping off rapid-fire barks. Glass crunched under its paws as it ducked and entered Left Coast.

"Shit, behind the counter—now!" Gillian yanked Troy back. Jeff chased after them and ducked. Gillian peered over the register. "Lydia, what the fuck?"

Lydia crouched and did a weird duck walk around a few tables toward the couches. A young boy in a chocolate-smeared Spider-Man shirt hugged his knees and cried next to a shelf of games. The werewolf's prowl stopped when it reached the stand holding sugar and creamer. It grabbed a metal jug and chugged. Lydia glanced back at Gillian and mouthed she was going to save the boy.

Gillian whipped her head in a that-is-the-stupidest-thing-I've-ever-heard motion, whispering, "It's going to kill you."

Lydia waved Gillian's concerns away. She was already so close and could probably make it back to safety before getting caught by the monster. Which was currently in the middle of the coffee shop, sniffing the air, tapping its finger claw against its thigh. Reaching a hand out, she locked eyes with the boy. "Hey there, what's your name?"

The kid rubbed his nose, leaving a streak of yellowish snot across his face. "Garrett."

"Alright Garrett, I'm Lydia. Why don't you come with me?"

A series of snarls, barks, and screams were the exact opposite of what Lydia wanted the kid to hear. The boy stared over her shoulder. When she checked, her hand shot up to cover his eyes. The werewolf pinned a plaid-wearing, wizard-bearded hipster against the counter attached to the front window. Claws shredded through flannel and flesh, spraying ribbons of skin and blood into the air. The beast snapped at the dude's face, nipping out chunks of fleshy cheek.

Lydia scooped up the boy and tried to hustle on her tiptoes. The process felt awkward and definitely looked silly. Garrett squirmed in her grip, he was a hefty boy and Lydia didn't have much experience picking up kids or sneaking past werewolves. She tried her best, holding the child like a plastic bag full of apples. Her calves screamed out. She kept her sight on the counter, repeating to herself that once she got there, she could drop the kid, and he could walk. The focus helped, for the most part, though his bowling ball head made her blind to the tables covered with mugs of coffee, the chairs strewn about, a garbage can. When this blindness caused her to bump a table and send a cascade of dishes crashing to the floor, she cursed herself for not being better at holding children.

"Oh shit," everybody said in unison.

Jeff waved at her to hurry up, Troy pointed at the werewolf as if she didn't know it was there, and Gillian searched behind the counter. A deep rumbling growl stretched into a poodle-esque yapping.

Blood, bits of fabric, and hipster chunks clung to the beast's fur as it locked her in its murderous sights. The monster hunched over, its broad fuzzy shoulders almost brushing the ceiling tiles. Lydia's bowels threatened to loosen when it curled its lip, spiked up the hair on its back, and prowled forward.

CHAPTER
NINE

LYDIA KNEW SHE SHOULD RUN. Garrett knew she should run. The monster knew she should run. Yet, her muscles wouldn't comply. Sweat dripped down her forehead and into her eyes. Her arms quaked from carrying the kid. Garrett pissed himself, soaking both of their clothes and stinging her nostrils. The werewolf swung and sent a table flying into a cowering woman. With another step, it loomed over the two, flashing its blood and flesh covered teeth.

Before it could strike, an aluminum pitcher smashed into the beast's snout. The werewolf yelped, covered its nose with a paw, and raised its tan eyebrows. Cream dripped down the side of its face, its red tongue slipping out for an exploratory taste. As it snarled and shifted to find who dared throw Half-and-Half at it, a napkin holder flew through the air and connected with its bicep. A canister of whipped cream came next. A cardboard box of utensils missed it by a mile, forks and spoons clattering across the floor. Troy cursed. Shrink-wrapped slices of banana bread slapped against the beast. It snapped at them, chewing and swallowing, its jaw hanging open, its tail wagging. The monster whined, begging for another treat.

As the coffee shop's makeshift weaponry whistled across the

open space, Lydia felt a tap on her shoulder. Jeff, holding a tip jar in his left hand, stood behind her. "Come on, they're almost outta crap to throw."

He wound back and tossed the glass jar like a hand grenade. Dollar bills floated out of it before landing on the creature's foot with a crack. It yelped and lifted the injured paw. All treats forgotten, it did a stuttering limp-jump at them, growling and whining whenever its foot touched the ground. Jeff shoved Lydia back to the counter and safety.

The monster swiped at Jeff, catching his sweater, and tearing a gash into his back. He winced and jerked his shoulder away, yelling at Troy to do something.

Troy scanned the bare counter, his jittery hands digging through drawers and shelves, coming up with nothing. Energy shot through his limbs, and he couldn't stop himself from grinning when he spotted a brown plastic bottle stuck behind the cappuccino machine. Troy closed his eyes for a moment, whispered a short prayer, and whipped it at the monster.

The nozzle top fell off, letting loose a stream of chocolate syrup. It sailed through the air, brown liquid trailing behind like a rocket's smoke trail. The beautiful spin was picture perfect. His smile melted when the bottle somehow found the thin space between the monster and ceiling.

Before Lydia or Troy or young Garrett could let out a string of curse words, the chocolaty afterburn splashed onto the monster. The beast's hairy arm paused in the air, it cocked its head, its jaw hanging open. Brown syrup dripped off its ears and muzzle, coating its nostrils and lips. Its growl morphed into a whine, and it stumbled back, pawing at the liquid.

"Guys, what the fuck are you doing?" Troy said.

Lydia didn't waste any time wondering if the monster didn't like being sticky. She tightened her grip on Garrett, bumped into Jeff because of Garrett's huge head blocking most of her view, and hustled to her friends.

They barreled through a brown double door behind the

counter and entered a hallway-like stockroom. Customers and employees huddled along the walls and next to metal shelves full of cardboard boxes and plastic containers. At the far end was a door Lydia guessed led outside.

"Hey, whose kid is this?" Jeff pointed to the urine-soaked Garrett.

A woman in an orange floppy hat and beige sweater raised her hand after a minute. The expression on her face showed a mixture of relief and disappointment as she stared at her boy. "Yeah, that one's mine."

"What the fuck, lady?" Jeff said.

Lydia pried the boy off her shoulders and set him down. As Garrett stomped toward his mom, he dragged his hand across a shelf, knocking over boxes of take-out cups and plates. The mom motioned at the boy with her palms out. "He's kind of a shit."

"Whatever," Jeff said.

Free of the extra weight, Lydia and Jeff joined their friends by the back door.

"What now?" Gillian said.

"That was pretty messed up, I can't believe my throw actually distracted the werewolf." Troy bounced and pumped his fist.

Lydia glanced at the cafe. "I really don't think it's a werewolf. I mean, come on Troy, you know they're not real. Maybe it's a dog or wolf with some kind of fucked up rabies?"

"That's crazy talk. What kind of rabies would make a dog look like a buff dude? Or cause it to walk on their back legs?" Troy touched his chin. "Though, it'd be pretty wild if it was rabies. Imagine if we got those rabies. Would we get all swole and tall like that? Or would we grow hair and start walking on all fours?"

"That's not what I...never mind." Lydia faced the others. "Do you think we're safe here?"

Jeff grabbed the back door's handle. "Whatever it is, though definitely not a dog or a werewolf, we just pissed it off. I say we head to my car and get the hell out of town."

CHAPTER
TEN

FAT GRAY CLOUDS rolled in from Lake Michigan. Wind investigated North Leeland with a hush. Waves crashed and beat at the coast in an attempt to claim more territory. Four friends huddled in the alley outside of Left Coast Coffee Works. They tried shaking off the horrors of what they'd just witnessed and the possibility that werewolves really existed.

On the left side of where the alley met the sidewalk laid a chewed-up torso with one arm attached. Intestines, bloody stomach, and a pinkish lung covered the concrete. Flies buzzed and gorged themselves on the buffet, not caring about the chill in the air when there's a free meal. Erratic red wolf-like pawprints circled the corpse parts and led across the street.

"Shit, I think that's Josh's shirt." Troy leaned against the wall, his head in his hands.

"Could this be from the monster in Left Coast? Do you think it's looking for us? Do you think there's more?" Lydia said.

Gillian scoffed. "What the fuck kind of question is that? You really think there's just a bunch of those things running around? Of course that's from the monster in there."

"I don't know, it's just..." Lydia scratched her arm and avoided her friend's face.

"It does look kinda fresh," Troy said. "But, there could be more?"

"I don't want to find out. Come on, I parked over here." Jeff hugged the wall as he crept away from the body that was probably Josh.

The alley took them past the backside of the coffee shop, a boutique, a real estate office, and another one of those crappy novelty tourist shops toward the south side of town. They did their best to stick together, though Jeff kept hissing at them to catch up. When he reached the edge of the building he stopped and backed away, his face contorted into disgust.

"What's going on?" Lydia said, peering beyond Jeff.

Gillian joined in on the scan. "Oh god, what is it? Is that thing waiting for us? Don't fucking tell me there's another one or a whole gang of—"

"I think it'd be a pack," Troy added. "Or maybe a clan? Could it be a gaggle? No, that's ducks. Yeah, it's gotta be a pack of werewolves."

Lydia's stomach roiled with acid. How could Gillian one minute laugh at the suggestion of more than one, and then the next minute ask that? Heat flushed her cheeks, and she thought about speaking, but kept it inside.

Gillian glared at Troy, her mouth open, her eyebrows scrunched up.

He shrunk. "Sorry. Continue."

"I'm just saying, what the fuck is happening?"

They all waited for Jeff. His shoulders heaved; his chest expanded. "I don't know if the same one ran through here or if somehow there's more than one, and I definitely have no clue what is happening. But..."

He gestured beyond the alley.

The side street they'd been aiming for contained bed and breakfasts, a couple of law offices, and random businesses that come and go; today it held the twisted aftermath of a werewolf party. Spatters of blood coated every surface. Coils of wolf shit dotted the sidewalks and street. An old man hung over a fire hydrant, his cracked-open head leaked brain matter on the side-walk, the bottom half of his spine poked out of his back. A young girl's blue checkered torso laid on a sewer grate, one of her legs leaned against a picket fence, the other leg in the middle of the street, her left arm on the front step of Emily's Bed and Breakfast, the right arm nowhere in sight. And in the middle of it all: Jeff's car.

"So, yeah…" Jeff said, his voice dripping with sarcasm.

"Dude, did a werewolf piss all over your car?" Troy pointed at the puddle of urine next to the tire, the glistening streaks cutting through the dirt on the side of his car.

The group slunk back into the alley. Jeff frowned, the street his sole focus. "This could be good or bad."

"I don't know, man, I bet their pee is super pee. It's definitely going to peel your paint."

Gillian slapped Troy on the side of the head. Jeff thanked her as he studied the ground, wondering if Troy was right about the paint—and, more importantly, what to do next.

The normally pleasant scent of Lake Michigan had been ruined with all the wolf shit and corpses. Lydia couldn't believe all the damage one of those monsters could cause. *Unless…* The thought hung there like her lingering hope of doing more than working at a shitty fudge shop in a shitty vacation town. *Was I right? Is there more than one?*

If there were other beasts, where were they?

Was that thing in the coffee shop what Winston had been obsessing over all these years? The question brought the old man to her mind and if he'd seen the beast today. Could he be dead? He was old, had a limp and an eyepatch, he'd be easy pickings for the monster. If her phone worked, she would have called him. She tried remembering where he said he was going, maybe they could save him.

"What are we waiting for? Your car is right there," Gillian said.

Jeff motioned at the leftover chaos like he was displaying a grand prize. "Whatever did this might still be around. I didn't want to run out there without knowing for sure it's safe."

"It's definitely a werewolf," Troy said.

"I still don't think so," Lydia said. Troy's knowledge must have come from the same movies she'd watched. And since no one really knew they existed before now, they were probably the best source for the famous monster. Yet, using totally accurate movie lore, most of what she saw in Left Coast didn't point to it being Lycan. "I always thought werewolves were night creatures, you know? And I don't know, shouldn't it have looked more…wolf-like?"

Troy shook his head. "That's just a myth. I read somewhere it's not always due to the moon cycle, sometimes they can control their change, and besides, it's a full moon somewhere. Also, what could it be? A dog that grew human-size? Those super rabies?"

Lydia shrugged. The whole "it's a full moon somewhere" bit didn't sway her. She was sure there were a few counterpoints to poke holes in the argument, she just didn't want to debate. "Maybe? But whatever, let's just hope we don't run into it again. Speaking of, let's run, right?"

"How about I sneak over there, back my car up to the alley, and you all wait…" Before Jeff could finish, the group booked it toward his Toyota. "What the fuck?"

The slaps of their shoes against the street ricocheted against the buildings. When they reached the car, everyone found a door. Wrestling with the handles, their hearts pummeling their ribcage, they found the doors impossible to open. Jeff held up the remote, cocked an eyebrow, and pressed a button. The car alarm honked and might as well have been a dinner bell; the flashers highlighted fresh human meat was up for grabs.

"Shit, sorry." Jeff struggled with the black plastic rectangle and its multitude of buttons. Locks clicked open and closed, the horn stopped and started.

"Fucking hell are you doing?" Troy hopped in place and tried catching the door when it was unlocked.

Lydia and Gillian didn't fare any better with getting into the car.

A chain of barking and the thump of hairy paws ripped through the crazy dance of unlocking the car and leaving. The friends all did comical gulps and pulling of shirt collars, praying it was a couple of inquisitive neighborhood doggies instead of what they knew it was. Sure enough, their prayers were not answered.

Six werewolves appeared in the side yard of a law firm, hackles raised, teeth gleaming, and growls rumbling. One spotted beast pointed a claw at the car then made a few hand signals to the others. A communal *oh shit* passed through the friends, quickly followed by, *fuck there's definitely more than one.* Lydia guessed they had about three seconds before they were torn to bits. She ripped the key fob away from Jeff.

The alarm went silent. The locks stopped their erratic dance. She tossed the key back to Jeff as everyone ripped open their doors.

They stared out the back window as Jeff slammed on the gas. The monsters were nowhere.

"Uh, we all saw them, right?" Gillian said from the front seat.

"Yes?" Lydia turned around, the houses blurring past her strained eyesight.

"Fucking yes, we did. We're not playing that mysterious did-we-or-didn't-we bullshit. We all saw those fuckers, no doubt about it. Six motherfucking werewolves in town. This is some next-level shit. Like, where the hell have they been hiding?" Troy vibrated in his seat.

Quaint houses with front yards free of werewolf chaos passed by. No one out raking or chatting or putting up Halloween decorations. No one screaming or running for their lives.

"Do they know about the monsters? Are they hiding?" Lydia said.

"I'm sure they are," Jeff said, not believing himself. He coughed and focused on the road. "Now, we just drive till we hit Traverse City and home. We can get help for the town from there."

"What the hell is that?" Gillian pointed, her voice dripping with panic.

An impenetrable stack of downed trees laid in a haphazard pile across Pine Street. The top of a green truck peered over the pile, a wispy tendril of smoke floating above. Lydia was sure she recognized the vehicle. The brakes of Jeff's car screeched as they skidded to a stop a quarter mile away from freedom.

CHAPTER
ELEVEN

WINSTON ATTEMPTED to crouch and stay hidden amongst shadows as he limped past the houses on the edge of town. Doors were open, yards tore up, picket fences knocked over. A running car blocked the sidewalk, a puddle of blood near the driver-side door. If he could prop his useless leg and use his left foot for the pedal, he could probably make it to his shop way faster than limping through town. Just as he attempted to get into the seat, cries and howls cut through the neighborhood, and he was positive he'd be a sitting duck for the monsters that had to be nearby. Ditching the car, he continued his trek. A buzz and rattle of a car's engine came from behind him and grew quieter. *Good luck going that way.* Blood slicked his arm, the bite in his bicep throbbing. He winced and kept moving.

Not that I want to say I told you so, but those fuckers should have listened to me. The years of ridicule he faced from the townspeople and police bubbled in his guts. They were positive he'd killed his wife. It was a tough argument considering he and his wife were alone in the woods, and he claimed it was a massive demon dog monster from Hell that'd attacked them. Who would believe that? Their first theory had been a couple's argument turned deadly. The police said there wasn't enough evidence to convict him, even if they tried like hell. So, to cover their butts they explored the possibility of a bear attack, because what the fuck was a dogman? It didn't matter what they said, though, because rumors were going to do what rumors did. Especially when he moved to town and opened the fudge shop. They thought he was there to make sure no one found any evidence, or he was a sicko and wanted to be near the scene of the crime. Everyone in town could burn in hell for all he cared.

Yet now he had proof. Fuck, the proof was crawling through town.

The chilly October air coming off the lake, bringing gray clouds with it, did nothing for the sweat coating his chest as he passed the houses, the Dollar General, and a Mr. Frostee. The weapons of chocolate in his fudge shop called to him, told him they were ready to kill these fuckers. Screams and animal-like rumblings forced him to pick up his pace.

Two silhouettes ran across the Cheese Man's parking lot. Their arms waved over their heads like inflatable tube men. They reached the sidewalk and steered their momentum in the one direction he didn't want: toward him. As they got closer, he could make out the panic on their faces, the dirty blonde messy bun bouncing, the jingle of a ridiculous amount of keys slamming against a leg, and the creaking of an oversized cell phone holder on the other.

"Oh God!" the woman screeched.

A black-and-white spotted dogman tore after them, yapping. Before Winston could warn them, it pounced on the man. Claws sliced through Carhartt hoodie and flesh as they plummeted to the sidewalk. The beast dug with fervor into the dude's back, ribs snapped, flesh and organs spilled everywhere.

"Frank! No!" The woman slowed and fell to her knees.

Winston dived behind a wooden fence surrounding an ancient service center. His heart punched against the cage of his ribs. His skin prickled. The wound in his arm pulsed. Behind him were growls, cries, the squish of soft flesh rent under sharpened claws.

"Come on, old man, get up. Get out of here."

The cries became gurgles. The growls changed to the lapping of blood. Winston didn't move. Nails clicked against concrete. The beast huffed and sniffed before trotting away.

Winston breathed through his nose, staring at nothing. Had he ever seen the couple before? Or did they avoid him and his store in the past? *Fuck them.* It didn't matter who the dogmen killed, as long as they stayed around enough that he could pump them full of chocolate. He slammed his fist on the ground and gritted his teeth.

Squealing tires, the roar of an engine and a crash pulled him back to reality. He peered through the fence. A gray car with peeling paint near the back tire had smashed into the eyesore concrete cheese block with an affront to nature fake mouse poking out of a hole. Next to the wreck, a man stumbled around while staring at the sky. Four people piled out, one of them familiar. Someone yelped, dogmen howled, and the group stopped moving. Winston ducked back behind the fence, not wanting to witness what was sure to happen next. Yet, a few moments later the group of people booked it toward the back of the buildings on his side of the road.

He stared at where the group had gone, not really caring what they did, but more as motivation to get his ass moving. *If those damn kids can be doing something, so can I.* He stood, glancing at the street and the flayed-open woman. Blood, flesh, fabric, and organs coated the sidewalk. Her skin reminded Winston of an inside-out rubber glove filled with tomato sauce. He shuddered, seeing Jenn's face superimposed over the woman. Grimacing, he pulled his focus away from the body and memories.

As soon as he passed who he assumed was Frank but was really just a dogman snack, a crowd of townspeople erupted into the street. They ran in every direction, their eyes rolling in their sockets, snot slicking their lips, urine coating their crotches. Behind them emerged a pack of dogmen. The monsters caught up with the mob in seconds, quickly surrounding the humans, howling and barking as they shredded flesh. Winston thanked Jenn for distracting the monsters, though he knew she definitely didn't intend for it to happen like this. For a split second he wondered if he was a terrible person, but the thought dissipated when he saw the shit storm of a massacre blocking any clear path.

Ducking and diving, he squeezed his way through the madness. A family—or, at least two adults and three kids in puffy coats, cutesy knit caps, cool dude sunglasses, and fake torn jeans, though the jeans might have been torn by the monsters, he wasn't sure—filled the gap in front of him, whimpering. Winston found a very small opening and sidled up against the storefront windows of Stu's Hardware, following it as it angled into one of those old-timey downtown entrances covered by the second floor and surrounded by display windows funneling to the shop's door. He waited by the glass door, hoping the bait—no, he meant *family*—would pass by.

Frenzied barking told him his plan half-worked.

Two muscle-bound beasts with pointed ears, brindle fur, and foaming snouts charged past his hiding spot. The family snapped out of their panic a moment too late. The dogmen used their jaws to clamp on to a kid, while using their arms to punch and puncture the others. In two blinks of an eye the family turned into exploded sacks of blood and goo and organs. The monsters dug into the feast, slurping and scarfing up the human cranberry sauce congealing on the sidewalk.

Winston took their distracted eating as his cue to get the hell out of there. He crept along the glass on his way to the street when he spotted a problem—or, more like three *big hairy* problems. A group of dogmen were prancing down the sidewalk as if they were shopping right where he needed to go.

"Fuck."

Winston backed up until he reached the hardware store's door. Locked.

"Double fuck."

Glancing around, he spotted a stack of paving stones near the entrance. *Damn, Stu is selling these for six dollars a brick?* Winston didn't feel too bad about what he did next. The glass shattered and was way louder than he thought it'd be. He jammed his hand into the hole, slicing his non-chewed arm in the process, now both limbs bleeding, and unlocked the door. As he crossed the threshold, hot gross breath blew onto his bare neck and a scratchy paw gripped his side.

THE WEREWOLVES MILLED about around the blockade of trees. Two wrestled, barking and nipping at each other's ankles. Some of them stood stock still, growling at Jeff's car, their fur spiked. Others pointed in different directions, nodding at specific werewolves and growling.

Jeff glared at their only way out, the things that'd been terrorizing them all morning. He punched the top of the steering wheel and hung his head. "We were so fucking close."

"Just plow through them. I'm sure we can make it," Gillian said.

"Maybe. Or we'd end up smashed against those trees like that truck there, and then the bastards tear into us like a can of dog food." He punched the wheel again. "Fuck."

"Alright then, what should we do? We can't just sit here," Gillian said.

They waited for Jeff to come up with a plan. He usually always had a backup and a backup to the backup. When Lydia had to cut down on classes due to work and not owning a car, Jeff worked out a schedule that let them all ride in together. Or the time he figured out how to get them out of community service due to their antics with a shifty fake teacher by wooing the school board. Sitting in the car now, staring at the blocked escape route, they were positive he had something.

"What if we went farther north?" Gillian said, tired of waiting. She glanced at Lydia and Troy for support. "Maybe we could hide somewhere near the beach?"

Jeff shushed her. "Just wait, I'm thinking."

"We need a shit load of silver. Then we could take the bastards out." Troy shifted forward into the space between the driver and passenger seats. "If I had a couple silver swords or bullets, I could tear my way through like a fucking ninja."

"That's stupid. First, where are you going to find a silver sword?" Jeff said. "Second, it's dumb."

"Whatever. It's better than doing nothing until we're a werewolf snack."

Lydia tapped her foot against the floor, her fingers against her thigh, and squirmed in her seat. She wanted to tell them they should go to the fudge shop and hide. Or go to the police station. They couldn't stay here, the monsters had to attack them at any minute, and the longer they sat there the more likely they were going to die. Instead, she increased her frantic tapping and waited for someone to come up with a plan.

The car's engine ticked, the howls and barks continued. A few monsters had lost their battle with patience and doggy training, and broke away from the pack. They stalked the car, their ears back, their teeth bared. If the friends were going to escape, now would be a good time.

"Okay, actually, I've got an idea," Jeff said.

"I'm sure there's somewhere up there we can hide—"

"No, hiding is a terrible idea. And there's nothing up there except rocks and sand and trees. The monsters wouldn't have any problems finding us. No, what if we got on a boat?"

Gillian shot a glance at Jeff that would have anyone questioning if it might be safer out with the werewolves than in the car with her. "What the fuck are you talking about? A boat? Where did this idea come from?"

Jeff shifted the car into reverse, gave it too much gas and whipped the vehicle around like he was one of the guys from the Fast & Furious movies. Gillian slammed against the car door, Troy and Lydia bounced off each other. "Well, going north would just trap us, right? And the only road out of town is blocked. If we tried to run on foot, we'd be like those people all over the street back there. So, our only option is the water."

Lydia had to admit it was a good point. Maybe a bit insane, and probably not what she'd do. It probably would make more sense to try to find a landline and hide. She knew none of them had a boat. And where would they even find one at this time of year? Her mouth went dry when she decided she'd speak up. But, as the words reached her lips, Gillian cut her off.

"I guess that's a good idea," Gillian said. "Do you even know how to drive a boat?"

"How hard can it be?"

"Don't like that response." Troy shook his head. "Oh boy, were in the middle of Lake Michigan stranded, having to drink our pee."

"Troy. We can drink the water."

"Hey wait, what boat? Last time I checked, all the boats were put up in the marinas. Unless you think a rickety fishing boat would carry us all?"

"The police boat is still there. So, here's the plan. We go to the police station, convince them to give us the keys to the boat, maybe some guns, then sail—or more like *boat*—to safety."

"Arc they really going to give us all of that? And what about the monsters?" Lydia said.

"I'm sure the werewolves can't swim that great. At least not as fast as a boat. And don't worry about the idiot cops, I can talk them into giving me the keys."

Lydia and Troy glanced at each other. If they had telepathic abilities, the conversation would be along the lines of, *This flimsy plan is shit. No way the cops are just going to hand us the keys. Jeff is slipping in his cool-guy-always-three-steps-ahead status. Should we say something?* Neither spoke up, because they didn't have telepathic abilities.

Jeff ignored stop signs as he sped down Pine Street, this time going north instead of south. Even though they'd just driven this street only a few minutes ago, the change caused them to gasp. Piles of dirt and grassy clumps dug up by the werewolves filled the front yards of many houses. A teenager lay tangled in his bike on the sidewalk, half of his face torn off revealing a blood-slicked skull, one of his eyes stuck under a tire. A few houses down was an elderly woman, her floral print muumuu shredded and covered in gore. More chewed and desiccated bodies were strewn about. Lydia covered her face, unable to take it all in. While she loved *Predator*, *Robocop*, and *Dead Alive*, seeing it in real life felt horrible. She urged Jeff to go faster.

"Holy hell, man, this is insane. How did they do this so fast?" Troy said.

"You saw how many there were, right?" Jeff said, as he swerved around a minivan half on the sidewalk and half on the road. Its windows were shattered, claw marks cut jagged lines through the burgundy paint, streaks of blood covered one of those stick figure family stickers.

"Where did they come from? No one noticed a bunch of werewolves in the wild? That's just insane," Gillian said.

Troy leaned between the front seats, serious. "I bet there's a secret bunker in the woods and someone was keeping these guys there. It's probably some plan to create an army of were—oh shit, watch out!"

A man stumbled into the road. He limped, dragging his left foot, as he wrapped his arms around his stomach, unsuccessfully attempting to hold his guts inside. His head was cocked, forcing him to study the sky and possibly ask whoever might be up there why this was happening to him. Jeff swerved to the left and smashed into a porta-potty-size concrete block of cheese with a plaster mouse poking out of a hole.

Reality blinked out.

Lydia woke up first. Glass collected on her clothes and hair. A sweet scent mingled with an acrid odor and a crisp fall breeze. She untangled herself from the space between the front and back seats, her neck creaking while her back throbbed. Gillian groaned and rubbed at a cut on her forehead, smearing blood across her skin, before struggling with her seat belt. Outside, the man who'd caused the accident continued to stumble around before his intestines splashed onto the street and he toppled over. The squelch of guts popping open woke the others.

"Everyone okay?" Jeff slurred the question.

Troy hacked and spat out a tooth. "I think I broke something."

"Can you walk?" Lydia said, as she slunk out and offered a hand to Troy.

He didn't notice her trying to help as he wiped the blood off his mouth and pushed his door open. He tripped out of the car, righted himself, grumbled a yes.

"Good, because we're not taking my car." Jeff had to slam his shoulder into the door to escape. "Damn this sucks."

Gillian slipped on an errant coil of intestine. She grabbed Troy's shoulder to steady herself, causing him to yelp, which brought about a chorus of barks and howls. Troy bit down on his cry and slipped out of Gillian's grip as everyone else pretended to be statues.

Windchimes clinked together, leaves danced across the street, a door creaked, the werewolves' cacophony hung in the air. *Any second now, they'll come charging down the road*, Lydia thought as she scanned the road.

Jeff snapped his fingers. "Hey, we gotta go, follow me."

The others whipped their heads toward him, their eyes doing horrible things to his face. Gillian put her hands out in a what-the-fuck motion, then pointed at the bloody street. Jeff shrugged and lifted an eyebrow in an exactly-they'll-be-here-any-minute expression. Troy waved off all the silent communications and swayed like a drunk over to Jeff. Sighing, Lydia and Gillian knew they didn't have any other options but to follow.

"We'll keep off the street, if that's what you're worried about. There's that path between the buildings and the drop off, it should be hidden enough," Jeff said, walking away.

Troy glanced around and gestured to a store. "Hey, we should hit up Stu's. Get some weapons."

They stopped on the sidewalk, a string of two-story buildings and awnings in front of them. To their left was the Cheese Man's shop, beyond that were some bushes blocking a view of Lake Michigan. Lydia glanced around, her skin prickling as if someone was watching her. All she found was the torn and exploded corpses of a man and a woman. *Oh shit did we kill these two? Nope, that must have the monsters, thank God.* The relief she felt at not killing these two soured at the idea of her being okay with all the death.

"It'd take, like, two seconds to get there," Troy said.

"Yeah, and we'd be in the open the entire time," Gillian said.

"Actually, it's a pretty good idea." Jeff nodded at Troy and Troy beamed. "Considering we're going to have to cross the square to get to the station, weapons might be good. But let's try the back door."

Dumpsters, ancient picnic tables covered in scratches and cigarette ashes, and crunched cans of Faygo and Bell's littered the path behind the buildings. They passed a metal door leading to a kitchen appliance store. A couple of broken pallets leaning against the wall, along with a barrel leaking a sludgy black liquid marked Stu's Hardware. The group crowded around the door.

"Okay, we run in and grab what we can, then get the fuck out," Jeff said.

CHAPTER
THIRTEEN

A YELLOWISH BROWNISH darkness greeted them as they piled in. Edges of boxes and shelves could be found along the walls. Ahead, an opening offered aisles full of tools, paint, and random house goods. The back door closed with a thud. The friends jumped and put up their fists. Once they were positive it closed by itself and wasn't shut by a monster or a drunken Stu, they slowly turned away from the shadows. They listened for any signs of a werewolf snooping around. Besides the muffled terror outside, the building seemed clear.

Jeff broke the spell as he whispered they didn't have a lot of time. Reality crashed down on them, the fact that they were running from monsters, werewolves actually existed, despite Lydia questioning whether they were actually werewolves, and they could only escape their death via boat. Tiptoeing, they made their way into the store. Jeff led the party, scanning shadows and corners for a possible ambush. He attempted pointing and putting fingers up in sign language no one could decipher. Frowning, and sagging his shoulders, he gave up. "Just be quick and quiet."

"Oh, and try to find anything silver," Troy said.

Lydia shook her head, whatever they found would be better than nothing. She didn't want to crush Troy, so she kept quiet.

The group spread out amongst the aisles. Scanning shelves of hammers, saws, screwdrivers, files, those hand cranked hand drills a Warner Brothers cartoon character would use, paint brushes, rulers, laser levels, and boxes of nails became overwhelming. Lydia scratched her arms as she took in all the options. She couldn't focus on one tool. How do you choose a weapon you feel confident enough to use and, at the same time, inflict pain on a giant wolf monster? Are you sure you can swing a hammer hard and fast enough to do some damage, while keeping enough distance from a beast that could rip through your face? What about a screwdriver? It's kind of like a knife. Again, you'd have to worry about getting in close and having the strength to puncture skin. A ruler is simply out of the question, as well as the paint brush, unless you had some silver paint. You could maybe stick the nails between your fingers and act like Wolverine. But that would mean having to punch and hope the nails don't move. Wolverine never has to worry about that, have you seen his arms? In the end, Lydia settled on a hammer, Jeff and Gillian picked up some screwdrivers and wrenches, and Troy held a silver doorknob and a pick ax in each hand.

"Nice call on the ax thing," Jeff said. "But what are you going to do with the doorknob?"

"It's silver, dude."

"Yeah, but what are you gonna do? Throw it at 'em? Fuckin' punch a monster with it, c'mon, really?"

Troy studied the hunk of ornamental silver in the palm of his hand. Besides the screw sticking out of the backend, it was smooth and didn't offer much in the way of damage potential. Though, it was silver and that had to've been like plus five in bonus damage. "I don't know. Probably throw it. This thing coming at your head, it's definitely going to hurt."

"Good luck with that." Jeff shook his head in resigned acceptance of his friend's crazy theories. "Time to go."

As Jeff went to open the back-office door, glass shattered at the front of the store. Something snarled and someone grunted before a full-on barking versus yelling match started.

"Fuck! They're here!" Gillian said, brandishing her screwdriver like a pro.

"We should probably help them." Lydia said. Her heart skipped a beat. Did she say that out loud before waiting to see what the others would say?

Jeff pulled the back door open as quietly as he could. A slice of light slipped in. "They might already be dead; we should just go."

Heat flushed Lydia's cheeks. Why did she suggest helping, Jeff was right. *No, don't second guess yourself.*

The monster yelped as more glass pinged and crashed to the floor.

"Ha! Take that, ya hairy bastard!" the grizzled voice roared through the store.

Lydia's ears perked up. "That sounds like Winston."

"Your boss? What's your boss doing here?" Gillian said.

CHAPTER
FOURTEEN

WINSTON CURSED through gritted teeth as he wrestled the fluffy dogman for control over the door to Stu's Hardware. Its claws bent the metal frame while it pushed and barked. His muscles strained, sweat slicked his forehead, but he pulled just as hard as the beast. The tug of war continued until the dogman put its full weight onto the door. Winston's boots skidded on the floor. It snapped at him through the opening. He reeled back, losing precious inches in the schoolyard battle for territory. Winston yanked on the door, throwing the beast off balance, then slammed it back on its nose. The crunch and yelp made him smile. It clawed at its nose and stumbled away from the door. With a shit-eating grin, he locked the door.

"Ha! Take that, ya bastard!" Winston put his hands on his hips and stared at the dogman. His joy disappeared when it snarled, sized up the door, and wound up to charge. "Fuck."

Winston limped deeper into the store in search for a weapon. He passed the hammers, saws, drills, and knives, and headed to the cash register. There he found what he needed. Glass shattered; a series of barks reverberated through the store. A shelving unit crashed down, sending nails and tools across the floor. Winston dug into the display of dark chocolate bars, ripping packages to shreds. He stacked them on the counter like stacks of gun magazines.

The slightly injured dogman scampered into the aisle. When it spotted him, it flashed its teeth, flattened its stubby ears, and growled. Winston grabbed two bars, snapped them into jagged triangles, and gripped one in each hand. He squared up with the monster.

"Alright you hairy bastard, let's do this." Winston grimaced, wishing he had said something cooler.

It charged, puffy hair waving, mouth open, tongue lolling amongst yellowish fangs. When the combatants crashed together, Winston's legs gave out and they tumbled to the floor.

Stars danced in his good eye; bolts of pain shot through his skull. Heat roiled off the monster. Its rancid breath coated Winston's tongue with the taste of shit and meat. He gagged while struggling to keep its jaws away from his face. The dogman pressed all its weight down on his glass-shredded arm and caused his elbow to screech out in mercy under the strain.

Fear coiled in his guts as it slashed his chest. He tried pushing the dogman up again, ignoring the agony coursing through his arm. Thrusting the chocolate towards the monster's mouth, he told himself he only needed to get it in there. The thing squirmed, its head never in one place. Each time he thought he'd succeeded; it'd snap its jaws centimeters from his fingers.

All the training with squirt guns he'd done, he never pictured this type of battle. Manic glee cracked his face when he decided his only option was to sacrifice his hand for a deathblow to the monster.

He waited for the perfect opportunity to jam his arm down its throat when there was a loud thud and the dogman grunted before falling over.

"Yeah, you got it, Jeff!" a deep voice said from Winston's right.

"Of course I did, Troy, what'd you expect?"

Four silhouettes faded into view as they charged forward. Two men led the group, one bigger than the other, brandishing a pickax, a wrench, and—for some strange reason—a doorknob. They dived onto the monster, stabbing and pummeling its body. A woman with dirty blonde hair and a green jacket circled the fight, grim determination on her face as she held a screwdriver like a knife. The dogman flailed, snarled, and snapped at the men. A hand came into view, one Winston instantly recognized by the silver rings on her fingers. Her usual spiky hair matted to her dirty, scratched face. "What are you doing here, Winston?"

"Lydia?" He didn't fight her when she pulled him up. He felt an urge to yell at her, tell her to get the hell out of town, and an unfamiliar need to hug her. Instead, he faced the battle. "They need my help."

"It's okay, they can handle it, I think. Are you okay?" She offered a sad smile, tightening her grip on his hand. The smile withered and she let go of him, staring at the sticky brown goo on her hand. She wiped it on her pants as her her nose crinkled, and she gagged. "Gross."

The two on the monster yelled, their weapons thudding against hairy flesh. Winston shook his head at Lydia's revulsion. He hoped they were actually hurting the dogman. Maybe the beast could be killed with regular weapons, probably not the doorknob, and chocolate wasn't their only weakness. Though, that would mean those years of being a weirdo in the backroom with squirt guns and chocolate were pointless. The monster cowered under their blows, yelping with each hit. Winston stared at his chocolatey hands and felt like an idiot.

One guy rubbed the doorknob against the dogman's chest. "Why isn't this working?"

"Gillian, stab it!" the smaller of the two men said.

The determined woman with the screwdriver, Winston assumed was Gillian, spoke to the others and they shifted, exposing the dogman's chest. Winston licked his lips, his good eye taking it all in. She screamed like a barbarian and brought the screwdriver down onto the monster's body.

The tool slid off its chest, the momentum sending the woman crashing into the humans and monster. The dogman shook them off before rolling over. It shot out a paw and dug its claws into the bigger man's calf.

"Fuck! Someone help Troy!" Gillian said.

"Winston, what are you doing?" Lydia said.

"Killing this fucker." He squeezed the broken chocolate bar and barreled into the monster. With all of his strength he wrestled Troy's leg out of the monster's grip. He didn't give Troy any time to recover, eyeing him and Jeff. "Pin it down but let me get to its mouth."

They stared at the old man. One steely gaze, one grizzled snarl, was enough to keep them quiet. The group's attack must have dazed the monster enough that it struggled to get up. Troy and Jeff wormed around on the hairy body, doing their best to avoid getting fur in their mouth, until they held it in place.

Winston kneeled and yanked the dogman's snout. It bucked trying to shake its head out of his hands. Jeff bopped it right between its stubby ears with his hammer. It blinked and slowed its movements. The pause allowed Winston to pinch the top of its wet nose. The beast grumbled and panted, releasing its noxious breath, but its dazed look and sluggish movements continued. Jeff's face turned green and gagged. Winston stared into the monster's eye. "Eat this."

He thrust the chocolate and his arm into its open maw. Once it was as deep as he could get, he released the melted bar and pulled his limb out before forcing the monster's mouth shut. Its eyes bulged, revealing the yellowish white parts. Its throat bobbed as it swallowed.

The dogman snapped to life and scrambled to stand. Swaying on its paws, it swung at the woman, missing her by a mile. Brown bits of drool clung to its furry jaws. The group circled it, ready to attack. Winston knew what was going to come when he saw its cheeks balloon, and stepped out of the splash zone. He told the others to get away. They didn't listen, so this was on them. Bloody chocolate vomit sprayed out of its mouth. Jeff won the gross lottery as the throw-up hit him right in the chest, splashing up on his face and down his legs. Instead of stepping a foot in either direction, he stood there and squealed as he was coated. The chunky goop weakened into a trickle. Once its liquid insides dried up, the dogman crumbled to the floor.

"What. The. Fuck," Troy said.

The woman with the screwdriver tiptoed to the vomit-coated Jeff, waving her hand in front of her nose. "Jeez, Jeff, you okay?"

Revulsion masked Jeff's face as he stared at the bits of dogman gunk stuck to his clothes. He ripped his shirt off, revealing a slightly tanned six pack. He dropped the shirt with a splat. "No, Gillian. No, I'm not okay."

Winston poked at the dead monster with his boot. *One more down.* His wounded arms were on fire, the cuts across his chest stung, his heart clunked and sputtered. The sooner he could get to his chocolate guns the better. Seeing how fast the dogmen died after being force fed chocolate gave him some hope. As long as he had decent aim it shouldn't be too hard to take them out.

"...did you do to it?" Jeff said.

Winston faced the shirtless guy with vomit on his cheeks. *Who are these people? What is Lydia doing here?* It didn't matter, he needed to leave.

"Hey, can you hear me? What did you do?" Jeff spoke slow and loud.

"I killed it," Winston said.

"Yeah, but how? Gillian fucking stabbed it with a screwdriver, and it didn't die?"

"I even rubbed silver on it," Troy added.

Jeff turned his attention to Gillian, a slight scowl on his face. "Did you miss it?"

"Fuck off. Why don't you find a shirt? No one needs to see that." She crossed her arms and glared at Winston. "But, seriously, how did you kill it?"

He leaned against the counter, waiting for his heart to slow. "Chocolate kills dogs. Figured it'd work on these dogmen bastards, too."

Troy scoffed. "Dogmen? That's ridiculous, they don't exist. It's definitely a werewolf."

A series of expressions passed over his face before he landed on understanding and he pointed at Winston. "Maybe it was a werewolf that killed your wife, not a bear or a dogman or you. I bet more people would have believed you if you said it was a werewolf."

Jeff grabbed a flannel jacket off a shelf. It wasn't his style, but it was cold out. "Chocolate kills dogs? You're insane. Obviously, it choked."

Winston pushed off the counter, his muscles thrumming with the need to punch the shit out of some kids. "Listen here, son, I've already killed one of these bastards. And if it wasn't for me, your pansy asses would've been dog food. And look at it—does it look like a fucking werewolf?"

"I mean, it kinda looks like a werewolf," Troy said, realizing maybe they were right.

"But, seriously, chocolate? I know it's not good for them, but kill them? Especially one that fucking big?" Jeff shook his head.

Winston once again contemplated punching this guy. "Clearly this fucking bastard is dead. And I don't know, I'm not a food scientist or dogman doctor. It works, and that's good enough for me."

"Guys, none of this is helping." Lydia stood between them. "We need to go. Winston, you should come with us."

"I'm going to the fudge shop," Winston said.

"What? Fuck, man, that's crazy." Jeff picked up a new hammer, then checked Pine Street through the front door. "It looks clear. We can get to the police station, get the guns, get the keys, and get the fuck out. You have fun at the fudge shop."

Meeting Jeff at the door, Winston shook his head. "Guns will do nothing. And if you are trying to get out of town on Pine Street, you'll have to go by foot."

Lydia touched Winston's shoulder. Her eyes were large. "We've got a pretty good plan; you should come with us. We can protect you."

Winston rubbed his face. "I don't want to leave. I want to kill these fuckers. And my stack of chocolate weapons is going to help me do it."

"What the fuck?" Jeff snorted. "Well, whatever. Good luck, old man."

"Jeff, he *is* old, we should take him," Lydia said.

Annoyance rumbled inside Winston's skull; he didn't need Lydia to stand up for him.

The others bounced on their feet. Winston glanced at them, counting the minutes they'd all last before getting eaten. "I'm fine. I'll do better than you all. You'd just slow me down."

Jeff raised his hands and cocked his head in an I-told-you-so gesture. "Great, it's settled. Good luck."

With that, Jeff opened the front door and left the others behind. Winston snorted and cursed when the group's de facto leader went in the direction he also needed to go.

CHAPTER
FIFTEEN

WINSTON WEIGHED GOING through the back, not wanting to lose this battle of wills, or dealing with this Jeff guy and his cocky attitude. Before he could stomp away, Lydia hooked him by the arm, careful to avoid the bite. She pulled him out the door to join the other plucky kids who were surely going to get Winston killed.

"Come on, this isn't the time to be your usual jerky self," she said. "Even if you can kill one or two, I can't imagine you being able to kill them all. You'll die."

She paused. This morning he was treating her like shit for showing up to work, and there were the countless times of getting chewed out before that. Why did she want to save him?

He snorted and yanked his arm away. "Trust me, those hairy sons of bitches are all going to die."

"Winston, that's crazy. There's too many. But, whatever." She put her hands up and slowly shook her head. "We're heading in the same direction, anyway. At least come with us part of the way."

Winston knew it'd be pointless to argue with Lydia. Her heart was in the right place. Grumbling, he nodded and let her lead him.

All five weaved through broken cars and half-chewed bodies. They did their best to avoid the massive piles of dogshit, which were everywhere. How could there be so much shit and how could it be stacked exactly like soft serve ice cream? Winston tried to avoid seeing North Leeland in shambles, trying to keep hold onto his hate for the town. Yet, Jenn loved this place, and since the dogmen were the cause of this chaos, he couldn't help being pissed. Lydia dragged him along. Troy and Gillian ran parallel behind Jeff, brandishing their hammers like crucifixes before vampires. He didn't want to follow them, even if they happened to be heading in the direction of his shop, they were slowing him down.

A low howl sauntered after them.

"You all gotta find a place to hide," Winston said.

"On it, old man," Jeff said, as he pointed toward a side street on his right.

Winston gritted his teeth and grumbled in his throat. *What if I used them as bait?* Some tiny voice buried deep inside told him that was a terrible idea. He countered it by saying he wouldn't actively use them that way, maybe Jeff, but if one of the others accidentally fell into a dogman's jaws or they didn't notice him leaving while they were in a dog fight, he wouldn't see it as a problem.

Jeff took a sharp turn onto Shady Oaks Court, a tiny street used for truck deliveries and avoiding Pine Street traffic. The boring dirty walls of brick buildings crowded the road. The others followed.

"Motherfucker," Troy said, as he skidded to a stop.

The group agreed, motherfucker indeed.

A RV, one of those Greyhound bus types that make you wonder if a hotel would be cheaper, blocked the end of the street. Smoke billowed out of its cracked black windows. The crunched front of the vehicle smushed up against the building on the left side of Shady Oaks Court. Bricks and debris littered the road near the front tires, fire and sparks popping and crackling from the engine. The vehicle's back end, and the only clear passage out of the alley, wasn't much better, with six dogmen tearing into a corpse.

Winston pulled away from Lydia and started back down Pine Street. "Well, good luck."

"Whatever. There's more than one way to the station." Jeff followed the old man, the others close behind.

They only made it a few steps when a roly poly brindle-colored dogman pranced onto the street near Stu's. A slick black-furred one with pointy ears and a miniature wiry one with floppy ears appeared on the street's north side, cutting off any escape. Six round eyes flashed fire when they spotted the group.

Winston cursed. Without the stupid limp, he could've probably put some distance between himself and the monsters. If he hadn't let Lydia pull him along, he could have at least grabbed some chocolate from the hardware store. He whipped around to tell Lydia off, but the group had returned to the alley, hiding under a rusty ladder attached to the left building's fire escape. His anger dissipated some, a bit of shame blossomed in his gut. He swallowed it down to let it boil in his rage and stomach acid.

Winston shuffled to the others as Jeff hung from the ladder, winking at the group before scrambling up. He jumped in an open window, then—after a heartbeat—stuck his head back out. "Come on, it's safe."

They glanced at the ladder; the first rung had to be ten feet in the air, and wondered how the hell Jeff jumped so high. Troy swore under his breath, positioned himself under the ladder and offered his hands for a boost. Gillian kissed him on the cheek before climbing, ignoring his grumbles of pain. Lydia thanked him and followed.

Winston weighed being trapped in an unknown space with these kids against his chances of sneaking past the dogmen. Their clicking claws and growls motivated him.

"You can do this, man, hurry up, my friggin' shoulder is killing me," Troy said.

It took an awkward second of bending his wounded leg and fumbling with Troy's head for balance. They figured it out and he grabbed the ladder. Blood streamed out of his bites and cuts, bringing waves of nausea and naughty language. A storm of pain thundered in Winston's head, he swallowed it down, gritted his teeth and climbed.

"Fuck!" Panic threaded Troy's voice.

The two packs of dogmen converged on Troy, yapping and snorting. He attempted a jump, his fingers touching the bottom rung, when a monster tackled him. The crack of his skull against concrete became a dinner bell for the beasts.

"We gotta help him!" Lydia said.

Dogmen piled on top of Troy. Their claws slashed at clothes and flesh. Blood showered the monsters. He punched at the wiry one, knocking it right in the snout. It whined and shook its head. He kicked and connected with the stomach of a golden-haired monster. The hit only caused it to latch onto his thigh. Troy screamed as it yanked back on his leg. The biggest dogman reared up with its paws and slammed into his chest and face, taking the fight out of him.

"I…" Winston trailed off, mesmerized by the brindle-colored dogman locking its jaws onto Troy's neck.

Lydia pushed Winston aside, holding a lamp in one hand and a stone award from the Chamber of Commerce in the other. She threw them out the window. The lamp smashed against the concrete with a pop, the award connected with a roly one, only causing it to pause in its chewing. Next came books, a Kleenex box, and a potted plant. She screamed at Gillian and Jeff to help. They tried, scrambling for anything that might hurt the monsters, yet they couldn't pull themselves away from their friend's attack.

The brindle dogman with Troy's neck in its mouth whipped its head back and forth. Troy gurgled and moaned, before a *snap* and the life left his eyes.

Lydia collapsed with a gasp. Tears streaked Gillian's pale face as she joined Lydia on the floor, wrapping her in her arms.

Winston glanced at them, then focused back outside. The dogmen made quick work of Troy's corpse, entrails being slurped, puddles of blood being lapped up, limbs chewed. *Fucking hell, I gotta get to my shop.* Sure, he felt sorta bad about them losing a friend, Lydia seemed really upset, and for some reason a twinge of indigestion burned his chest at the sight of her. But he couldn't waste time worrying about her or the others, he had a mission and it didn't include taking care of some kids. Which led to how the hell was he going to get out of here?

CHAPTER
SIXTEEN

THE ROOM they were holed up in was a combo kitchen, dining area, and living room, with scuffed hardwood floors, pictures of Lake Michigan on the walls, and an overstuffed couch. Lydia and Gillian sunk into a depression in the cushions, holding each other and crying quietly. Windows on the wall opposite of him revealed the town square. Jeff was digging through the olive-green refrigerator. Pizza boxes and dishes were piled on the counter. Two doors marked the edges of the kitchen.

One of those might lead out of here.

Winston dug through the kitchen drawers. He only needed a bit of chocolate to arm himself before leaving. All he found were mismatched utensils, cords, papers, random batteries, and takeout menus. He set aside a few band-aids he found. A cabinet was full of vanilla protein shakes, vanilla wafers, vanilla flavored cereals, and vanilla covered pretzels. He slammed each one closed, frustration curling his toes and grinding his teeth.

The clatter brought Jeff's head out of the fridge; a bottle of beer stuck to his mouth. His eyes were red. Wiping his mouth, he banged the bottle down. "What the hell are you doing?"

Winston growled and continued his search.

"Dude, what's your deal?"

"Don't worry about me. Why don't you pull your head out of your ass and go check on the ladies?"

"Fuck off, man. I'm giving them space." He took another pull from the beer. Rubbed his eye. He stared at nothing and sniffed. "I don't know what to say, and I usually always do. Troy was my friend. He made things lighter, and I don't know how to do that. He could make you laugh and show you the world wasn't always shit. But, fuck, what the hell?"

Behind them, the girls sniffled and sobbed. He felt a slight pull at his heart strings for Lydia. The dogmen's howls came from outside. Winston stopped digging through the drawers and sighed. *I should have gone right to one of these doors and got the fuck out.* Giving a pep talk or consoling grieving people was not in his wheelhouse.

"Troy seemed like a good guy. But listen, you gotta stay strong. This is a good spot to wait it out." Winston passed by Jeff, almost patting the guy on the shoulder, and went to a door. "I'm going to go out there and stop this."

"Staying here isn't an option. You've seen those bastards; they can get into anything. No, we're going to go there." He went to the window and jabbed a finger at the police station. "My plan is a good one. We need to get out of here and on the water is the best way."

Winston stared at the dozens of dogmen filling the square. His eye drifted down Pine Street toward his shop. He could feel it waiting for him.

How the hell am I going to pass those hairy bastards without them noticing me?

Lydia and Gillian joined them at the window. Mascara streaked Lydia's face. "Why is this happening? We were supposed to just be hanging out."

She gave Winston guff, but always in a fun way. They actually joked together a few times. She never dug deep into what he did in the backroom or pried into what happened to Jenn. He liked listening to her tell off annoying customers or noisy townspeople. And there was comfort in having her at the counter when he ventured out of the workshop. She wasn't so bad. He snorted and avoided looking at her, not wanting to follow this trail of thoughts any further.

"Just stay here, Lydia."

She shook her head. "That's crazy, you shouldn't be alone."

He let it go, not wanting to argue.

"Who's going to tell Troy's family?" Gillian said, using her sleeve to clean her nose.

"Won't you? I mean…" Lydia said.

"I, yeah, I guess I probably should." Gillian's face flushed and she turned to wipe her eyes. After composing herself, her eyes burned with determination. "Where are the police? Shouldn't there be a bunch of cops running around or, I don't know, the Army?"

"I have a feeling their bodies are on the street," Winston said, "or they're hiding like pansies in the station. And who in the government is going to believe a bunch of dogmen are attacking? They didn't believe me when I told them. Those bastards said I was crazy. Well, look what's happening now."

Jeff snorted, his face tight. "Oh right, you've dealt with this before. You've faced off with these *monsters* years ago and since we didn't listen, we laughed, this is the payment, right? We're all just idiots?" He stomped away from the window. "Guess it feels pretty good being able to gloat that you didn't kill your wife. You are just—"

Winston's fist shot out faster than anyone expected. The crunch of Jeff's nose preceded the spray of blood. Jeff stumbled into a cupboard, sending dishes to the ground.

Winston rubbed his hand. "I didn't kill my wife."

"Fuck man, what the hell?" Gillian puffed up her chest and raised her fists.

Lydia jumped between them. "Guys, this isn't helping."

The howls and barks masked the silence in the apartment. Time slowed to the speed of that one old man driving down the street always in front of you when you need to be somewhere. Gillian glared at Winston, ignoring Lydia's pleas to chill the fuck out. Jeff sniffled and held his nose. Blood dribbled over his lips.

Winston put his hands up, palms out. "Look, I don't want to fight any of y'all. I didn't mean to hurt your friend there, but he can't talk about my wife."

"Dude, we get it. But you can't go around punching us because you're pissed. Especially right now." Lydia pointed at the dogmen. "There's bigger issues right now."

The old man nodded and offered Jeff a scrap of a paper towel. "Sorry. How's your beak?"

Jeff glared at him, then wiped his face. He shrugged. "It's not too bad, for a lucky punch."

The tension in the room fizzled. No one really wanted Winston with his full rage on. The speed of the punch was like Rocky taking down Thunderlips Hulk Hogan. Plus, they were all pretty positive the old man was insane and would murder them if provoked. These thoughts joined their weighing exhaustion. Lydia sunk onto the couch, holding her head in her hands. Gillian helped Jeff search the kitchen for food. Winston stayed by the window, patching up the bite on his arm while studying the dogmen outside.

"Okay, so…" Jeff said.

His words floated through Winston's ears as he tried to figure out the best way to get to his shop. While coming up with a strategy to sneak back to the trail behind Stu's building and ignoring the fact he'd have to pass in full view of those monsters hanging out in the grassy area, he noticed how some of the dogmen stood in a circle. Their heads bobbed and their jaws moved. A spotted one pointed at thin brown dogman, shook his head, and the others actually slapped their knees and bent over in what appeared to be laughter. *What the fuck are they doing? Talking?* Footsteps creaked in the apartment, a door squeaked open and closed.

"…let's go." Jeff finished.

"I still think it'd be better if we stayed here, or maybe," Lydia glanced at Winston, "went to see what Winston has in his shop."

"We literally just talked about this. We are doing the boat thing, and that's it."

The others nodded and lined up by the door near the fridge. Lydia didn't move, her jaw tightening. Her shoulders sagged, resignation on her face, and joined the group. Their bloody exhausted faces turned to Winston. Whatever plan Jeff had come up with was probably terrible. Jenn would probably not be too happy with him leaving the group to their fate. She'd say, *Hey old man, it's not about you, it's not about me. Stop being such a stubborn idiot and help those kids. Also, maybe don't use me—* Winston brushed the thought away and clung to his need to murder all the dogmen.

He readied his future response to Lydia for when he left them all on the street. He held onto a sliver of hope she'd survive. The hope burned like indigestion, and he wondered if he was getting soft.

Lydia placed her hand in Winston's. "Come on, it won't be much longer until we're safe."

CHAPTER
SEVENTEEN

THE TIGHT STAIRWELL to the shop squeezed them and squeaked with each step. Winston thought they were ringing the dinner bell for the monsters. Sweat and stale air stunk up the space. He felt contained and itchy, his hands balling into fists, his muscles begging to be used for death dealing. Should he have told Lydia she was a good employee, that his leaving them to die wasn't a reflection on her? The words were on his tongue. He swallowed when they reached the wooden door at the bottom.

Jeff held the handle. "Okay, be ready for anything."

Really? This is his big plan? Winston shook his head.

When Jeff opened the door, they all held their breath. Instead of a torrent of barks, of claws digging into Jeff's body, of game over, they were met with a cheerful pink flamingo floatie. "Well, alright, that's not so bad. But, still, be careful, the monsters could be anywhere."

They filed out of the stairwell and into an assault of garish color and bright lights. Cheesy t-shirts with slogans like "I like beer," "Panty Inspector," and "Take my wife, I'd rather be fishing" lined the walls. Michigan hoodies, pants, and tie-dyed clothing filled the cramped racks in the cramped space. Umbrellas and beach toys hung from the ceiling. Shelves were jammed with shitty memorabilia and tchotchkes no one would ever buy. The air held the scent of coconut lotion and burnt apples from the candles on a rack near the cash register.

Weaving through the overabundance, Jeff and the others held tight to their hammers and screwdrivers, their heads on a swivel. No one called out saying they found blood or a dead body or a pile of shit. Winston pushed past the group and aimed for the register. While digging through colorful boxes and displays filled with foil and paper wrapping, the friends reached the door.

"Hey, what are you doing?" Gillian said.

"Getting weapons." Winston grabbed handfuls of Halloween chocolates, a couple of boxes of Whoppers, a few bars of chocolate. His pockets bulged and crinkled with enough candy to carry him through his plan.

Jeff scoffed. "Fine, whatever. Just hurry up."

Winston really hoped a dogman would eat this guy.

If they ignored the bloodstains, random limbs, dropped purses and backpacks, coats, trash, and piles of poo, Pine Street seemed safe. No dogmen waiting for the group, no panicked people cowering or crying, no apparent danger to stop their plan.

The calm made Winston check his weapons and made his scalp tingle. They were right next door to the town square, and the grassy yard had been turned into a friggin' dog park. The bastards should be bounding around the street, ignoring any rules a park for dogs would have, because they were dogmen not dogs that follow rules. Which meant they must be waiting for the group. He didn't like the idea that the beasts were intelligent enough to create an ambush.

The four moved without speaking. Running in a line, they bounced from shadow to shadow. Winston limped along as fast as he could. When they came up to the side street where Troy died, Jeff whisper-yelled at them to go faster. He led them down another block and Winston put together they were taking a side street that'd avoid the town square and get them closer to the police station.

Despite himself, he had to admit Jeff had a good plan.

More bloodstains marked their path, chunks of flesh on the sidewalk acted as sign posts. A man's decapitated head watched them run. Lydia slowed. "This is terrible."

Winston caught up to her. "Hey, just don't look—alright? You're almost there."

"But all these people…"

"Were assholes. And look, I know you all want to get help, so better them," he pointed at the corpses, "than you. Think about all the other people you're going to save. We're going to stop this. But you gotta keep moving."

She stared at him; disgust painted on her face. He wondered if he should have kept some of that inside. Lydia increased her stride.

Jeff rounded a corner onto Marigold Trail. The group could make out the police station's gray facade only a few blocks ahead. When they passed the Pizza Brick, their run slowed to a jog, partly to let Winston and Lydia catch up.

"Okay, let's all just stick close," Jeff said, between labored breaths. "We can get in through the side door. Beat any monster back for now. Once we get the guns, we'll show those bastards a thing or two."

Winston wanted to tell them for the millionth time guns would do nothing. Instead, he decided this was a perfect opportunity to disappear. As soon as the three entered the town square the dogmen would be all over them, then Winston could slip away. He didn't want to admit it, but this path and their distraction was much better than what he originally mapped out. A pang of indigestion spiked his stomach when his gaze fell on Lydia. He shook it away, telling himself maybe she'd survive, and followed the friends on their way to their soon-to-be death.

Halfway down the street they neared an alley with two dogmen sniffing around a corpse. Jeff pointed across the road at one of the small trees planted along the sidewalk. Everyone gave him a how-the-fuck-is-that-tiny-tree-supposed-to-help expression. He squinted at them and frowned, then with complicated hand motions tried to explain how the monsters appeared distracted and might not notice. His friends didn't understand. Lydia growled and glanced at Winston, frustration plain on her face. Jeff put his middle finger to his lips, communicating what he thought about them and to be quiet at the same time. That worked. As stealthy as they could be, Jeff and Gillian hustled past the alley, leaving Lydia to help Winston limp along.

Confidence flowed through them when the dogmen didn't react. The clear path promised an easy passage to the police station. However, as the saying goes, they shouldn't have counted their eggs before the chicken laid them, or the one about how not every dog has its day. Barking and howling shredded their hopes, and those hopes were pissed on and set on fire when the dogmen in the alley responded. Adding to the pile of dashed hopes were the group bounding into view at the end of the street at the same time as the alley dogmen slunk out and boxed the group in. The confidence flowing through the group became a stream running down their legs as they faced the flaw in Jeff's plan.

JEFF BROKE AWAY from Gillian and picked up the pace, either ignoring the monsters or wanting to surprise them with a full-frontal assault. A gray and black shepherd dogman, slobbering and barking, barreled toward him, not falling for his trickery. When the beast was within reach, he swung his hammer. Its blue eyes went cross from the smack against its skull, and it stumbled. The monster responded by cutting jagged wounds across Jeff's back. Yelling, he kept running, eyes on the prize.

Close behind the action, Gillian poked the monster with her screwdriver. The blade didn't break any skin on its arm, but it delayed the beast long enough for her to get away and follow Jeff.

Winston puffed and cursed his bum leg as he hobbled after the others. His vision wavered, his arms felt like he'd been in the shop mixing fudge by hand all day. Stinging pain highlighted his bleeding wounds. He pushed through the need to stop when he heard the alley dogmen stalking and growling at his heels. He fumbled with the box of Whoppers, keeping an eye on Lydia in front of her. She glanced back and saw him slowing down. "Come on, hurry up."

"I'm…fine…get to your friends," he said, tearing the box top off with his teeth.

"Damnit, give me one of those." Lydia stuck out her hand, accepting a chocolate bar with only a slight grimace and gagging sound. "I can't believe they took off without us."

The two humans were armed and ready when the alley dogmen, a gray mess of folds and a silky long-haired red one, met them on the street. The monsters yipped and gnashed their fangs. Winston and Lydia, being much cooler, simply nodded. The epic battle commenced.

The old man struck first, juking and jiving as he put some distance between him and his super wrinkly enemy. He dumped some Whoppers into his palm. Ignoring the throb in his injured arm, he threw them like tiny baseballs while continuing to move. Each chocolate ball bounced against the ripples of fleshy gray fur on the monster, without getting so much as a twitch out of the creature. Candies rolled around on the street between them. He cursed and emptied the box, continuing his backwards progress. The monster shortened the distance, its pudgy ears pulled back, its curly tail straight out. Then its legs began sliding and kicking out like a chorus line dancer, chocolate candy marbles sliding under its feet. Its arms pinwheeled before it took a comical prat-fall, yelping when it hit the ground. The beast lay there groaning. The fudge shop owner took advantage of the situation, wound up a softball pitch and underhanded the round chocolate at the monster. The dogman yelped and shot back up on to its feet as he took the chocolate right in the eyeball.

It wiped at the melting chocolate ball, cracking the Whopper into annoying little pieces. The bits liquified and were absorbed into its eye goo. The beast shook its head and whined, swinging its paws at invisible foes. Winston rushed the beast and emptied his handful of chocolate down the creature's throat. While the gray monster died vomiting red and brown blood, Winston searched for Lydia.

He didn't like what he found.

The glamorous red-haired dogman with its snooty snout had her pinned to the road. Cuts and blood coated Lydia's body. She pounded the monster's luscious locks with one of her fists while with the other she tried jabbing the chocolate into its maw. Curses and screams poured from her mouth.

Winston watched the panic oozing from Lydia, glanced at Jeff and Gillian down the street and the monsters they were dealing with. This was his chance, what he'd been waiting for. The indigestion reared its ugly head again. *Do I really want to be a hero?* He didn't sign up to save these kids. Lydia might have been a faithful employee, but wasn't she there to keep the customers busy? She wasn't his child, wasn't his Jenn. Besides, he didn't want to go to the police station, that was Jeff's plan. If they were this close and he was the one being attacked, would they have stopped to save him?

Lydia would have.

She screamed as the beautiful monster dug a claw into the meat of her arm.

Fuck.

Winston wrapped his taut oak-like arm around the beast's surprisingly delicate neck and yanked. The monster gurgled and released Lydia. Three jagged trenches leaked dark blood down Lydia's bicep. Winston grunted as the beast raised, lifting him into the air, its locks tickling his face. As he hung from the creature like a JanSport backpack, he reached into his pocket. The wrapper crinkled with promise. He pinched and pulled the bar out of his pocket. A spark of glee flashed through him. The excitement dissipated when the monster swung an arm and knocked the chocolate to the street. Panic flared until he squashed it and jabbed a thumb into the monster's beautiful eye.

The beast, with its human JanSport, stumbled backwards. It whipped its body around to shake Winston off. He tightened his grip around its neck. They reached a wall, and the dogman slammed Winston into it over and over. Stars danced in his good eye, his grip on the reddish locks weakened, the world went wiggly. As he slipped off the dog show-prepped beast, it twirled and caught him. Murder flashed across its black pupils.

The position sent his mind racing back to the first time he encountered a dogman. The rough bark of a tree digging into his back. Excruciating pain as a claw gouged out his eye. Jenn's lifeless body crumpled and bloody on the dirt.

Winston blinked away the tears. The memory shifted and morphed. His wife's corpse disappeared, and in her place stood Lydia.

Blood dripped down her arms, her shirt darkened in patches. She bared her teeth as she slunk up behind the monster. A jagged bar of chocolate stuck out of her right hand, her leather belt in the left. She reached up and jammed the candy deep into the dogman's snout. The beast's eyes bulged as it cocked its head. Lydia flicked her wrist, and the belt whipped around its muzzle. Faster than Winston could comprehend, she cinched the belt tight. The monster dropped Winston and clawed at the makeshift bind, whimpering at its failed attempts to escape. Lydia shot her hands out, connecting with its soft neck, and dragged them down. The bulge of chocolate traveled down its throat. Brown drool leaked out of its black lips, trickling out of its nostrils. The creature fell to its knees before toppling to the street. It spasmed a few times then stilled.

"Thanks," Winston said.

Lydia kicked its still-gorgeous-even-in-death body. Her shoulders heaved a few times before she collapsed. Winston caught her, stopping her head from smacking into the concrete. They sat together, catching their breath. *She saved me.*

Winston's body cried out in pain. Despite all the training, he'd gotten old. He hated his body for that. There wasn't time to rest. Somewhere in the back of his head, Jenn told him to save the others. Whatever was hurting him had to wait until he was dead.

He pushed to his feet. "We can't stay here. But we should probably wrap your arm first."

Lydia groaned as she stood. Winston tore a strip from his shirt and tied it around the cuts in her bicep. While he finished the decent job of first aid, Lydia's wheeled around spotting the others battling their own dogmen. "Fuck, we gotta save them."

A skirmish waged in Winston's mind. The two sides argued the merits of disappearing or staying to fight. Should he attempt to take these other monsters down or save what chocolate he had left to protect him on his way to the fudge shop? With the beasts fighting Jeff and Gillian, there was a chance he could escape. Lydia stared at him, her pleading gaze agitating the indigestion in his chest. He glanced at the battle at the end of the street. Killing a dogman was killing a dogman. Did it matter if he did it now or later? He focused on the creature Lydia killed. The one that could have finished Winston off.

Fuck it.

CHAPTER
NINETEEN

WINSTON AND LYDIA limped down the street like a couple of desperados—only, instead of revolvers, they were armed with bars of pure chocolate.

Jeff had his dogman—a gray and black spotted number with pointed ears and stubby snout—cornered, pummeling its body with his hammer. The monster flicked its ears, whined, barked short, annoyed barks, snorted, and attempted to shake off the ineffective attacks to escape. Every time, Jeff swung his weapon to keep his combatant in place and bring about a string of pissed off yaps.

In Gillian's case, she was the one being cornered. Her monster must have been sadistic because it took its time slicing and clawing at her, barking in a staccato rhythm that could have been mistaken for laughter. Blood gushed from the various open wounds in her body. Her screwdriver hung limp at her side. She swayed; acceptance plastered to her bloody face.

"Shit!" Lydia said as she picked up her pace, wincing at her own injuries.

She almost made it.

The dogman tore its clawed Gillian's neck. The monster howled as Gillian's eyes rolled back, her head falling back and opening a jagged red grin below her chin. Her screwdriver slipped from her hand and clattered to the sidewalk. Opening its jaws, the dogman dug into the wound. Blood squirted and splattered, an awful lapping followed the snap of bone and tendon.

Lydia released a guttural cry and charged. Winston cursed, hobbling as fast as he could to catch up. When she got in striking distance, she lobbed the bar of chocolate over the dogman's head. The candy landed with a plop into the bloody opening in Gillian's neck. Winston appreciated the throw, though he thought her aim needed some work. Yet, the frenzied state of the dogman gorging itself kept it from noticing the chocolate. The beast continued chewing, slurping up Lydia's weapon without stopping. Lydia glanced at Winston and gave him a is-it-going-to-work look. He shrugged. The monster stopped mid-bite, its body jolting before it began hacking and holding its stomach. Bits of Gillian's flesh spewed out of its mouth.

Winston dug through his pockets for more chocolate. Lydia held her hand out, doing her best to ignore how gross the melted brown goop looked and felt. Armed, they trudged closer, slowing when the dogman clawed at its throat and fell to its knees. They nodded at each other in a fuck-yeah motion as it died in a horrible amount of stomach pain.

"Nice kill. Now, let's see what we can do about Jeff's hairy friend," Winston said, surprising himself.

Jeff's weak-ass slow swings, pathetic breathing, and the dogman's barking laughter all pointed to Winston and Lydia getting there just in time. The two flanked man and monster as if their minds were synced. Winston pushed Jeff out of the way and bearhugged the beast. It snapped at his face. He cackled as he dodged the attack, reeled back, and headbutted it in the snout. He wasn't sure who it hurt more, whose bones snapped, but at least it briefly stunned the creature. Lydia snaked her hand out and smeared melted chocolate on its lolling tongue. The monster narrowed its eyes at Winston, a slight head tilt at the thought of someone touching its tongue. Winston winked, hoping the monster knew it was a wink and not just a blink due to the whole having one eye. Either way, he felt pretty good about his team-up with Lydia as the creature snorted and hacked. Tears streamed out of its black eyes and its cheeks bulged.

"Lydia, close its mou—" A stream of dark brown vomit blasted out of the dogman's mouth and right into Winston's face.

Slick and slimy goo coated Winston's nose and cheeks, dripped into his gaping mouth. An awful mix of sweetness and acid, and chunky bits melted on his tongue. He gagged, his throat constricted, his stomach churned. The rush of bile and half-digested breakfast raced up his esophagus, exploded out of his mouth and onto the dogman.

A trail of chocolaty mucus hung between them. Winston's throat burned, sweat slicked his face and mingled with the monster's spit. The two stared at each other, trying to decide which was grosser. To be honest, Winston didn't care, all that mattered was his vomit had great aim and mostly entered the creature's mouth. As fast as he could, he released his bearhug and forced the monster to swallow his chocolate-coated vomit.

"What the fuck? God, that was horrible," Lydia said. She leaned against a building, gagging before releasing her own stomach contents onto the sidewalk.

Winston pushed the dogman over. It fell in a heap, clutching its stomach. He hawked a loogie and spit onto the creature's prone form. "Tell your friends where you got the fudge from."

"Dude, that was a weak one-liner," Jeff said, as he cleaned his chin, a puddle of his throw-up next to him. "Also, fucking disgusting."

He let out a breath and collapsed next to a dumpster.

Indecision kept Winston from jumping to either survivor's aid. Lydia wiped her mouth and said she was fine. So, he knelt next to Jeff. Streaks of blood painted the man's pale face. Cuts and tears crisscrossed his chest. He sat up with a grunt and waved Winston off.

"I didn't really have time to think of anything, maybe next time," Winston said.

Jeff laughed. He cut it off when he scanned the street. "Where's Gillian?"

The name hit Winston in the stomach, he totally forgot. Lydia sucked in a deep breath and cried. He hung his head, surprised by the feeling of loss. Another tally mark against these bastards. He opened his mouth, yet there were no words.

"God dammit!" Jeff buried his face.

"Come on, son. We can't stay here. More will come."

"Fuck this." Jeff struggled to his feet. He swayed for a moment. Glancing at his hands, he balled them into fists and steadied himself. A bit of sunlight broke through the clouds and hit the sweat on his body just right, like he was a bloodied mall mannequin. "I'm going to get every fucking gun out of that building, and I'm going to send every one of those fucking mutts to doggy hell."

"No Jeff." Lydia's voice stopped Winston and Jeff. "This idea is stupid. The chocolate works, let's go to the fudge shop and get loaded up and kill these fuckers."

He glanced at her, tears streaming down his cheeks, then glanced toward the town square. He released a howl and took off for the police station in a full sprint.

CHAPTER
TWENTY

JEFF'S INJURIES didn't slow down his manic, arms waving in the air, howling, erratic dash to the police station. Lydia took off after him. Winston blinked, unable to process what was happening. A curse escaped his lips as he hobbled behind Lydia. In the distance, dogmen did their dogman thing in the town square, sniffing butts and digging holes. It wouldn't take much for them to hear Jeff's screaming insanity or Lydia's rapid-fire footsteps.

"Lydia, hold up!"

She didn't stop, her focus zeroed in on Jeff. Huffing and puffing, pushing his bad leg, Winston continued to chase. He slowed at the sight of a dogman at the edge of the town square pointing at Jeff. Lydia skidded to a halt and checked if Winston saw that human-like gesture from the monster. He nodded and caught up to her, Jeff temporarily forgotten.

Two dogmen split from the doggie hole digging contest, glanced back at the pointing dogman, then charged toward the police station.

"Jeff." Lydia yelled. When he didn't change his mad dash, she turned to Winston with concern on her face. "What are they doing? And why do they seem smarter than they look?"

"I have no idea. Maybe that's the 'man' part of dogman?"

While this was happening, Jeff's progress was not great. Every few steps, his injuries caused him to stumble, or his body jerked in a random direction, as if the controller for his character was unplugged and he kept glitching. He eventually made it into the station, yet it seemed like hours after the dogmen did.

"We gotta stop him before they kill him," Lydia said as they jogged to the town square.

"Lydia, I'm sorry, but I think he's a lost cause. You see that look in his eyes?" Winston said.

She stopped and stood in front of Winston. Her voice was steel, something he'd never recognized in it before. "No, I'm not losing another friend. You and I are going to stop his sorry ass and we're going to your shop."

"I—"

"Nope, no arguments or excuses. You can't be as big an asshole as everyone thinks. You had plenty of chances to run, but you didn't."

He didn't mention he tried, and the dogmen kept stopping him from leaving.

"You're not going to give up and run away. I know you. You never give up. So don't give up on me or Jeff." Lydia thumbed her nose and faced the police station.

The indigestion he'd been feeling earlier flared up in his chest. Tears welled in his eye. *Those were Jenn's words.* She was absolutely right. He couldn't give up. "Alright, fine—"

The station exploded.

CHAPTER
TWENTY-ONE

A CLOUD of fire erupted where the building had been. Bricks, wood, glass, donuts, cute coffee mugs with sayings like "Police do it by the book" and "Why talk when a club can answer" flew into the town. Windows in the surrounding buildings shattered. The ground shook. Winston stumbled and fell; Lydia fell on top of him. The dogmen howled and scattered. Some were blasted to the ground, jagged bits of wood bounced off their fur. Car alarms squealed. The fire ate through any chance of salvation the station might have promised.

After a few minutes of dazed confusion and worries about brain damage, hearing loss, and singed clothing, they recovered enough to sit up. Scanning the damage led them to spotting Jeff sprawled on a patch of muddy grass halfway across the square. Lydia crawled to her friend. Winston gave her the time she needed, focusing on the dogmen shaking off the blast's effects.

Lydia screamed and held Jeff. Half a revolver had been lodged into Jeff's blackened chest; the chestnut handle stuck out like a tongue between his two nipples. Blood dribbled out of his mouth. Lydia squeezed one of his hands. His perfect blue eyes stared at the sky.

"What the hell? What. The. Hell. How? Why?" Lydia wiped her eyes. "You asshole. Why didn't you listen to me?"

Winston's vigilance weakened. They were just kids. They didn't deserve to deal with the pain he had dealt with. He realized how much he cared for Lydia. He should have seen it sooner. He should have shown her what he was doing in his work room, why he was prepping for the monsters. Winston reached out and laid his hand on her shoulder.

"Lydia, I'm sorry. I'm sorry for not thanking you for dealing with me. You were always good to me. You always cared." The dogmen's breathing and rumbles prickled Winston's senses. "It's time to go."

For a moment she did nothing. Her focus glued to Jeff's body. The last of her friends in town. What could she do now? She gritted her teeth. The chocolate worked. Winston was right. And he said he had weapons. Revenge. That's what she could do.

Long-haired pointy-snouted ones, meatball smushed-nose ones, trim muscular ones with shark smile jaws, and a few spotted ones formed a loose circle around them. Winston wasn't sure if the fire kept them from attacking or if they were savoring the moment. Smoke billowed up and darkened the sky, adding to the dread in town. The heat from the fire teased and warmed his skin. His pockets grew damp, the aroma of melting chocolate wafted around them. The beasts pawed at the dirt and growled.

Neither group broke the standstill. There were lots of teeth gnashing and deep grumbles, paws stomping the ground, but everyone stayed. A light brown short-haired monster with a curly tail squatted and dropped a turd. It then proceeded to scratch and kick the dirt behind it. The breeze played with the smoke, blowing it around the square, clouding the buildings. Winston calculated his options. The shop was probably three blocks away. Which didn't seem bad until considering the scores of monsters between them and their goal. He studied Lydia. Her eyes burned, her mouth a straight line of determination.

"Are you packing?" Steel coated her voice.

Winston stuck his hand into his pocket and came out with a palm of liquid chocolate. He showed it to her; she grimaced and turned away.

The lack of having any weapons was sitting in his stomach like the greasiest blob of cheese from the dirtiest pizza place in town. If he let it, it'd turn to shit or make him throw up. They weren't near a store he could snag chocolate from, or a sixty-year-old woman's purse full of "emergency" bits of chocolate for those midday cravings. The curly-tailed dogman inched closer, its ears down, the fire reflecting in its eyes. *Maybe we can toss a stick and see if the bastard would search for it?* It was a stupid idea. He faced Lydia, his chocolate-coated hand out in a any-ideas-on-how-to-get-out-of-this gesture.

She grabbed his sticky hand, not understanding his message, then pulled her arm back and made a gagging noise. "Ugh, melted chocolate grosses me out. It's like baby poo."

Winston rubbed his face, dumbfounded. Chocolate streaked his cheeks and forehead. "What the hell are you talking about?"

"It's just gross." She grimaced at her hand and attempted to wipe it off on her clothes. Streak of melted brown goo mixed with the blood on her shirt and pants. "I've always hated it."

"But you work at my fudge shop. There's melted chocolate everywhere."

She shrugged.

It struck him he'd said a similar thing to his wife. *Is this your idea of a joke, Jenn?*

The dogmen jostled each other and whined. A few pawed at their noses. A refrigerator-size fluffy one attempted to charge Winston and Lydia. It skidded to a stop, gagged, tucked its tail between its legs and shuffled backwards to hide behind the curly-tailed dogman.

"What's going on?" Lydia said out the side of her mouth.

"Maybe it's the fire?"

She smirked, her glance bouncing over his face. "Shit, we're covered in chocolate! Maybe the smell is freaking them out."

"Or they realize our bodies are tainted and could kill them."

The fire crackled, the wind whispered, the dogmen grumbled and barked their frustration. Lydia grabbed him by the elbow and dragged him toward the shop. The beasts whined, growled, and yapped, yet gave Winston and Lydia space.

The two hobbled through the pack of dogmen—Lydia's grip tight on Winston, pulling him along. Anger and murder and pain floated through their minds. Winston cracked a grin. Two heads truly were better than one. And two bodies strapped with chocolate were perfect for dealing death to these fucks.

CHAPTER
TWENTY-TWO

THE DOGMEN DIDN'T SIT IDLE LETTING their prey waltz by like it was cool. They barked deep barrel-chested barks, whined ear-piercing whines, and howled frustrated howls. Some spun and took off in random directions. Others scratched and pounded at the dirt. Spit and foam flecked their snouts. Furry fingers were pointed. Eyes glinted with anger. A few didn't care about the humans. They wanted to tear things up, eat fresh meat, and claim territory. But these two awful smelling humans were striking an instinctive nerve in all the dogmen.

The two humans did their best to outpace and escape the monsters. Lydia kept pulling Winston along. Pain spiked his knee and raced up his thigh, his arms were tired and sore. Ignoring it all, he focused on the strength she had hidden from him for a year. All the time working together and the bullshit he dealt her, he should have known. Pride and shame blossomed in his chest. When they got out of this, he'd treat her better, he'd even give her a raise.

A long-haired brown and white dogman trotted up to them. It snarled and dove at Winston's leg. Right before it hit him it skidded to a stop. Yelping, the monster scratched at its pointy snout. Another one bounded forward, its reddish wiry hair and floppy ears bouncing, and pushed the first one aside. It kept pace with Winston and swiped a claw at him, tearing out another slice of arm flesh. He grimaced, yet the day's adrenaline helped him ignore the searing pain. If a dogman could smile, it would have, instead it did that thing dogs do where they pull up their upper lip and lower the bottom lip, revealing closed teeth, and squinted its eyes. Shaking his head, Winston barked at the creature. The dogman's expression melted into pulled back ears, hurt in its eyes, and a slight doggy frown. *What did I say?* Anger bristled the beast's fur as it snapped at him. Before fangs tore into flesh, the poisonous aroma slipped into the monster's nostrils. Jerking its head back, it attempted to shake the terrible chocolate smell out. The frustrated pack slowed.

The block of buildings housing his shop resembled a beacon ahead. Bill's store and the realtor place that sold overpriced plots of land were busted-out shells of their former selves. Broken glass and chunks of wood littered the street. A circle of carnage surrounded the untouched Winston's Fudge Shop, a bubble of safety holding the lingering scent of overcooked fudge. Indigestion burned Winston's chest seeing Bill's place torn up.

"We're so close! Come on, old man, let's go," Lydia said.

Dogmen followed at a safe but threatening distance. A terrible musk of bloody fur, shit, and urine surrounded the beasts. The constant panting of all those monsters together drilled into Winston and Lydia's ears. It spurred them through the final push.

When they entered the store, Winston locked the door. None of the dogmen ventured beyond the sidewalk. They nipped each other, peed on the debris, and chased their tails.

"Well, if we needed another example of your theory working." Winston motioned out the window.

Lydia smirked and put her hands on her hips. "I'm a fucking genius."

"Yeah, yeah." Winston chuckled and limped to the kitchen. "We probably shouldn't count on it for too long. Let's get the weapons, clean up our wounds, and take these hairy bastards down."

Lydia went to her usual spot behind the counter. She grabbed a water bottle from a hidden shelf and chugged half of it down. Drool slicked her chin, mixing with the chocolate and blood on her face. "Okay, so seriously. These things are fucking real. And you actually ran into one before?"

The question caught him off guard. He stopped, his focus drifting toward some glass shelves on the wall. Boxes of chocolate Easter bunnies and creme eggs collected dust on a shelf. It'd been a while since he told the story. Too many people ridiculed and called him crazy. He always assumed Lydia knew, and well, at the time of hiring her, didn't want to have to go through the interview process again. The past tugged at his memories.

As he dug out bandages, disinfectant, and ibuprofen, he began to speak. "It was ten years ago; my wife Jenn and I were camping a few miles away at the State Park..."

"Do you really not know how to make s'mores?" Jenn laughed as she tossed a bag of marshmallows at him. A streak of late fall sun cut through the canopy of leaves, falling on her as if she were a goddess blessed by the heavens. "It's literally the easiest thing to make. Like three ingredients, a stick, and fire."

Winston picked up the bag, plastic crinkling in his manly hand, the puffed cubes of sugar popping back to their original shape. He beamed; a twinkle of light danced on his perfect teeth. He took in the sight of his beautiful wife in her red and black flannel, the top two buttons undone, exposing enough cleavage to leave him breathless. The crisp air played with her silver hair, as if God was trying to flirt with her. He flexed his bulging muscles and eyed the sky with his two very real eyes, daring God to try—

"Okay yeah, we don't have time for this," Lydia said.

"But you asked. Don't you want to know how I got this?" Winston motioned to his eye patch. "And how I figured out the chocolate would work?"

"I mean, I do. But not if you are going to tell it like some cheesy romance story. And bulging muscles? Come on. Besides..." Lydia pointed out the window. Three dogmen were acting like they were in an argument, complete with wild gestures, puffed up chest bumps, and head waggling. "Seriously, what the hell?"

"I'm really not sure. Like I said, I think this is the other side of them."

Lydia scrunched up her face. "So, kinda like how Bigfoot seems intelligent enough to not get caught?"

"Probably?"

They spent a few minutes finishing up wrapping their wounds. Winston dug through a fridge and some leftover Chinese food. He collapsed into a chair and closed his eye, the container of noodles instantly forgotten.

"Hey man, are you okay?"

"I just need a minute."

Lydia scarfed down two cold eggrolls. "Okay, let's say they have a bit of human intelligence. But, for the most part they are kinda crazy wild dogs. Was it the smarts side of them that decided to attack the town? Did they blow up the police station?"

"I honestly haven't given it much thought." Winston grumbled and grunted the words. He dumped a handful of ibuprofen into his mouth and chased it with water. Most of the pain he could ignore, the rest he prayed would go away so he could finish killing the fuckers. "I mostly focused my research on finding them. The reports were pretty vague on how smart they were, though I guess smart enough to stay hidden for years."

"That's fair. And I bet it was mostly vague stories we've heard a million times about every cryptid.

"Pretty much."

Lydia paced, checking the window for what the dogmen were doing. They were still milling about, though the three arguing were now sniffing each other's butts. "Then why come out now?"

"Maybe the BBQ? Or the siren? Or they were bored running around the woods?"

"I can maybe buy that."

Color returned to Winston's cheeks. He winced only a little when he dug in to eat. While swallowing food, he swallowed the pain. *I'll feel it when I'm dead.* A very manly way to handle it. "I'm still not sure on the police station blowing up. I'll have to think about that one."

"Actually," Lydia put up a finger. "I bet they either did something dumb on accident, or it was the dumb cops rigging the doors to blow up."

"Fucking cops."

After he emptied the container, and wiped grease from his lips, he stood. "Let's focus on those furry fucks. The weapons are in the back. And we can get back to my story I can tell you more of the story as we get ready." Winston shuffled to the backroom.

"Oh, that's okay. I don't need to hear it."

They cut through the kitchen and headed to the door with all the warnings. Lydia's curiosity lit a fire in her. A few locks were turned, a knob was rotated, and he stepped aside. Lydia tilted her head much like the dogmen had done. Winston grinned and gave a slow nod.

"So, uhm, that's a lot of weird looking squirt guns. What exactly are we going to do with them?"

Winston deflated. "We're going to kill those monsters." He cleared his throat and puffed up his chest. "Let me show you."

Wood workbenches full of 90's color palette tubing and pop-like canisters forced them close together as they squeezed their way into the room. Lydia spied the pots of liquid chocolate and heaved, backing into Winston. She swayed from nausea and focused on the pages and pictures taped to the wall. The crude drawings of dogmen made her laugh. She pointed at one of his targets, shaking her head at all the marks around the clean bullseye. Winston coughed and found some dirt to focus on.

"So, as I was going to say before being interrupted, when the dogman attacked me and my wife, we were making s'mores—"

Lydia traced a finger along a gun's barrel. "Yeah, yeah. I got it. Chocolate. Dogs. Unabomber making killer squirt guns?"

He plopped down onto a stool and chuckled. "Fine, I get it, you don't want to hear it. I just haven't been able to tell anyone how I got to coming up with these bitchin' death dealing weapons, I guess I'm just excited about using them."

Lydia picked up a contraption that had three upside down glass beakers attached to the top of a thick tube-like rifle barrel. She squinted down the sights at a target. Squeezing the trigger, a stream of hot chocolate smacked the bullseye. "Hey, no judgement here. You do you. It just explains why everyone thought you were crazy buying all this shit up. But, definitely not complaining right now."

"Those idiots would never have thought about the chocolate thing."

The gun drooped in Lydia's hand. "Let's not call them idiots. A lot of people died. No one deserved that."

Winston lowered his gaze. Jenn would have said the same thing, then smacked him upside his head. "You're right. Sorry."

She hefted a pack onto her shoulders. "It's fine. So, how about we get some revenge?"

Before Winston could get up, Lydia's eyes went wide, and she rushed out. Confusion twisted in Winston's gut. She returned with a black rectangular speaker and her phone. Pushing a button on top produced a beep. A few minutes of scrolling and she smiled. "We need some kickass montage music while we load up."

"Sure, montage music."

Direct Hit!'s "Werewolf Shame" blasted out of the box. Lydia closed her eyes and bopped along. Winston grimaced. *What the hell is this?* If this got her in the mood, then whatever.

Lydia put a hand up for him to wait. What they were waiting for, he had no idea but trusted her to have a reason. While he waited, he glanced at his weapons. Did he have enough? The weird looks he got buying all the squirt guns from Meijer and the Sandcastle Toy Store kept him from going back every other week. He never thought there'd be this many dogmen, never imagined there'd be a town full of monsters. Punching his thigh, he told himself not to worry. With Lydia here, they would figure it out.

Once the chorus hit, Lydia smirked at Winston. "Oh yeah, let's do this."

Music pumped through their heads, choreographing a wicked montage. They melted chocolate. They filled canisters. They stuck guns into pockets and makeshift holsters. Lydia only gagged a few times; Winston took over the melting and filling. She found a strip of red and white ribbon used for gift wrapping and tied it to her head. Backpacks were strapped to backs. Chocolate splashed onto pants and shoes, gummed up the floor, and stained pieces of paper. Winston's heart chugged along to the music's beat, a wicked smile glued to his face.

Lydia stood at the entrance, weapons and stains coating her body. "Why did I think all of these straps and belts would be easier to walk with? Yeesh, chocolate is everywhere. You ready?"

The picture of Jenn on the wall beamed at Winston. He touched her cheek with a chocolate-stained finger and bowed his head. "It's been a long time since I first came across one of these monsters. They took my wife and my life. In their place was a new purpose, to prove they existed with their dead corpses. Jenn, it's going to be over soon. I'll really be free now. I love you, dear, maybe I'll see you in a bit."

"Uhm, did you just call me Jenn? Also, you love me?" Lydia smirked.

Winston's mouth hung open. Red flushed his cheeks. "Wait, what? No. That's not…"

Lydia laughed and patted him on the back. "I got you, you crazy old man."

Outside the shop, howls and thumps of dogmen grew closer. Lydia toyed with the modified squirt gun. Winston took a deep breath and faced her.

They could do this. He had no doubt he needed her. Two people in sync as they were, there'd be no problem killing the monsters. Maybe this was Jenn's doing. Maybe Lydia stepped through his door and took the job for this moment. The dogmen took their lives away today. Now, they'd be unstoppable.

"Let's fuck shit up," Lydia said.

CHAPTER
TWENTY-THREE

FOR TEN YEARS he'd dreamed of the moment he actually got to use his weapons. All the preparation, all the solitude, all the burnt chocolate was for this opportunity. Winston didn't waste time worrying if they'd work. The squirt guns were ready. He was ready. Simmering rage had been kicked up to a high boil and the only way to release the pressure was to blast as many fuckers as possible with liquid chocolate.

The two busted out of the fudge shop with guns squirting. Hot chocolate streaked through the air. The dogmen's focus jumped between themselves, the humans, and the liquid flying toward them.

Then the chocolate hit.

Some of the stream splashed into the monsters' mouths, while others received a brown shower on their fur. Those with the chocolate surprise in their maws yowled and snorted, lashing out at whatever was close. Innocent dogmen were smashed into, chocolate splattered and smeared onto each other. The ones that weren't victims of the rage yipped and charged.

Winston and Lydia did their best facing down the frenzied beasts. Lydia split from her boss to cover more ground. All the while she kept her finger on the trigger of her flamethrower-like squirt gun, coating anything nearby. A slight tugging pulled at Winston's chest, and he wondered if he should stay close to her. Not that she needed the protection—the yelps and falling bodies proved she could handle herself. In the end, he decided she had a good idea about spreading out so they wouldn't be boxed in. He scurried in the opposite direction, leaving Lydia to deal out her destruction.

Winston fired his squirt guns with wild glee. Each shot found its mark, sending the monsters down gagging on chocolate. He stood his ground in front of Bill's shop. The beasts were a storm of fur and claws. Cocoa traced deadly arcs through the air. Pride and revenge coursed through his veins; the guns were doing exactly what he knew they would. The death surrounding him was glorious. Winston's laughter echoed off the walls.

As the dogmen squirmed on the ground, throwing up and dying, he took a chance and glanced over at Lydia. She had gained a crowd.

The squirt-thrower backpack made Lydia feel like a complete action movie badass. A high-pressure stream of chocolate cut a brown line through the monsters around her. The dogmen whined and yelped as the liquid poison sliced off fur, poked eyes, and punched stomachs. She had to give it to Winston, he knew how to convert a child's toy into a deadly weapon. At least for dogmen, kids would probably be pretty excited for a squirt gun that shot chocolate, Lydia wondered if they should market this afterwards. Giggles and "hell yeah"s burst from her as she stepped farther onto the street.

Sleek, tall, gray dogmen with whip-like tails and pointy snouts formed a group and charged. They pulled some wicked maneuvers—twirling, diving, and sliding to get through her defenses. Behind them came a few burly brown and black monsters, panting and pausing in a move Lydia believed had to do with a lack of exercise. She didn't have much time to consider the finer points of dogmen workouts before she was surrounded.

Lydia squeezed the trigger tighter, gritted her teeth, and aimed the gun muzzle-height. The plan blossomed in her head, and she knew she was a genius. The monsters didn't scare her, not now. All she felt was a need for revenge. These fuckers took her friends, her town, and deserved everything she was going to give them. She let them surround her. In a flash, she spun, becoming a chocolate dispensing star at the center of a dogman universe. She imagined Troy pumping his fist, Jeff nodding in approval, Gillian giving her a thumbs up. The air around her filled with steam, chocolate, monster fur, and lots of vomit. Lydia continued to spin; joy plastered on her face.

Steam floated above Lydia's backpack. *Maybe I should go help her?* A massive dogman stepped in front of Winston and changed his plans.

The beast rippled with muscle, teeth, and pissed-off energy. Gnarly white scars cut jagged lightning bolts across its bulging pectorals. A piece of broken metal poked through its pointed ear. The dogman flashed its red-stained fangs. Before Winston could squeeze his trigger, the monster slammed into him, knocking him on his back. He turtled, the backpack digging into his skin and stopping him from rolling over. The dogman pounced and straddled his body. Lowering its snout, it snarled in his face. Rancid shit breath made him gag.

"You shit-eating fucker!"

A choking gurgle bubbled out of its mouth in the dogmen's strange laughter. Winston punched the creature in the gut. His knuckles cracked and popped against the rock-hard stomach. The creature responded with another bout of its dog laughter and offered its rebuttal with a claw right to his chest. Dark blobs exploded in his vision. Blood squirted and soaked his shirt. Coughing, his lungs clunked and rattled. He rode the wave of pain while he dug into his side holster and attempted to push the monster away at the same time. The dogman leaned all of its weight onto his arm. A tunnel of darkness edged his sight. Each breath shallower than the last. Biting his tongue, he forced himself to stay conscious. He yanked the pocket-size gun out. Energy crackled through him. He offered the monster a bloody grin as he jammed the squirt gun into the creature's mouth.

Chocolate bubbled out around the plastic muzzle and fangs. The dogman reeled back, brown liquid dripping down its lower jaw. With the weight off him, he squirmed out from under the beast. The street rolled beneath his shaky legs. Fighting the vertigo, he leveled his weapon at the kneeling dogman.

"Hey, ugly, how about you try the hot chocolate?"

Finger squeezed trigger, plastic creaked, chocolate flowed through tubes to nozzle, and Winston's special formula drowned the dogman.

There wasn't much time for rejoicing while the beast released a stream of vomit. The pack charged. Winston sidestepped and fired. The backpack's weight lessened. He rushed the monsters, ignoring the slashing claws and snapping teeth. Every shot blasted one in the mouth. He kicked and tripped anything near him. Something hit him on his patched eye side and he stumbled.

A nail sliced his bicep and sent searing pain up and down his injured arm. Teeth and jaws latched onto his calf. Little animated black and white spotted dogs ran in circles around his vision. The world tilted. Winston growled and attempted to take a step backward only to have his leg slip out from under him. He landed with a crack and the imaginary mutts morphed into stars.

The dogmen piled on top of him. They scraped and nipped, yelped and barked, and squirmed to cover Winston. Heat overwhelmed him, sucked the breath out of his lungs. Furry faces and yellow fangs filled his sight. Drool coated his skin. Nasty-ass dog breath fogged his brain. Pain wracked his body as the monsters jostled each other for a better position. Fighting through the panic and cloudy thoughts, he pulled out two small chocolate squirt guns.

In a glorious explosion of chocolate and anger, he blasted the pile of monster flesh. He jabbed the deadly children's toys into open mouths, filling the throats with killing chocolate. Those that got a muzzle full of brown goo fell off him and spewed blood and cocoa. Flashes of blue sky broke through the dog monster bodies. Yet, more dogmen filled those gaps and closed off his chance for freedom.

The new monsters learned from their idiot brethren and kept their jaws locked shut, using claws to shred his body. A beast's wet snout smacked his cheek, clicking his teeth together. Rage filled his vision. Vengeance swallowed the pain. He thrust the gun's nozzle into the black void of a nostril and fired. The dogman's eyes bulged, a mucousy stream of chocolate leaked out of the open nose hole. It shook its head and clawed stripes of hairy flesh from its snout. When it fell over twitching, Winston howled and cackled.

While Winston acted like a crazy person, Lydia released a stream of curses. Each swear word of unimaginable filth was a bullet point to her situation. Her backpack squirt-thrower was releasing a pathetic tinkle of melted cocoa. Sweat coated her back, her skin burning from the heat radiating off the tank. Dead dogmen boxed her in. Her boss was either screaming or laughing as a pile of monsters squirmed all over him. Finally, the super gross and disgusting fact she had brown goo—Winston could go fuck himself with his thoughts about melted chocolate —all over her and none in her gun sunk in.

On the positive side, at least most of her dogmen were dead.

She weighed the options of saving him right away or picking another group of bastards to attack. He could probably take care of himself—that sound he was making had to be laughter. Besides, there's plenty of dogmen running around. No, she told herself, it can't be good to be under a pile of monsters, he definitely needed her help.

Taking careful steps, she attempted to not slip on the melted chocolate, blood, and vomit. She kept her eyes on the pile of dogmen covering Winston as she climbed over a brown and white wrinkly mass. Her foot touched something squishy, she yanked it back, causing her to tumble sideways.

"Motherfucker!" she said as she pinwheeled her arms. Searching for more solid ground only led her to slipping on a limp dogman tail. Her body twisted, the backpack throwing her off balance, her spinning arms useless. One of her hands hit the body of a furry white dogman, which helped gravity win out and bring her down.

She registered the puddle of chocolate before she could react. The splash of melted brown candies was worse than the time she got soaked on the log ride at Michigan's Adventure. Her stomach churned, her throat restricted, her mind revolted. The chocolate touched her tongue and she kept thinking about loose baby poo. Coughing and choking, she scrambled to the side and bumped into a pair of hairy legs. Bulging, fuzzy shadows loomed all around her, one raised a muscular arm then slashed it down.

A quiet scream cut through his victory. Ignoring the dogmen surrounding him, he scanned between stocky limbs and found the source of panic. A pack of monsters had Lydia pinned to the ground. She struggled with them, her gun farting out a weak brown cloud. The beasts howled and piled on top of her.

Anger crawled up his insides and pushed away any rational thought. If he'd listened to heavy metal, a cacophony of double bass drums, shredding guitars, and vocal-cord-tearing screams would have blasted through his head. But he didn't. So, it was a sort of static, a sea of scrambled TV signals occupying his brain.

From some place above, he watched himself explode to his feet, and become a viking, Arnold Schwarzenegger, one of those guys from the movie *300*. He jammed pressurized turkey basters full of sloshing chocolate into snouts, into eyes, into pointed ears, into one unlucky asshole. Brown goo leaked out of every orifice. Cries of pain and rage filled the town, coming both from the monsters and Winston. Piles of dead dogmen filled the street. He was chaos, a tornado, a chocolate cloud of death.

When he came to his senses, he found himself in the town square. A shallow layer of shit, piss, blood, and chocolate coated the streets. Spatters of gore clung to the buildings. A miasma of sick hung in the air. Winston collapsed into a puddle on the grass.

"I fucking did it. I fucking killed them all."

What was he supposed to do now? All these years and it was

done. No longer did he have to worry about the monsters hiding in the woods. He didn't have to build any more weapons, or deal with chocolate and fudge. He could rest now that he accomplished what he promised Jenn at her funeral. He could do what she would want him to do: be free.

The longer he sat in the puddle, the more exhaustion weighed on him. Silence comforted and lulled him until he could barely fight sleep. Something gnawed at him, something he was missing. A vision of his shop floated through his mind. Why? There was definitely something important he couldn't place, that worried him.

"Crap."

He jumped to his feet. His mind rewound the battle. A single frame came to the forefront, of Lydia being overwhelmed by the monsters moments before he went full-on barbarian.

"Motherfucker!"

CHAPTER
TWENTY-FOUR

PANIC SEIZED HIS CHEST. The success meant nothing if he lost Lydia. Who cared how many dogmen he killed if his partner wasn't here? Tears dripped down the cheek underneath his good eye. He wouldn't have been able to do this without her. Any of this.

Age hung and pulled on his shoulders as he stared at where she had been the last time he'd seen her. The area was littered with dogmen corpses. But no sign of Lydia anywhere. Did they eat her? Did they take her? He had no idea why they'd kidnap her. In the little time he'd interacted with the monsters they seemed more interested in killing. Still, he prayed this was something new and there was a chance.

He limped over to the spot, hoping to find anything that might give him an answer to what happened. Dogman bodies were splayed out around a human-sized space in the middle of the road. Chocolate vomit trickled out of their mouths and mingled with some splatters of blood. Her squirt-thrower backpack was missing. They couldn't have eaten that. A blossom of hope appeared in his gut.

"Lydia?" Winston searched the buildings and the trees. "Lydia!"

Car alarms honked in the distance, the faint whisper of Lake Michigan's waves, the rustle of leaves, but no response. No dogman barks or growls. No beasts charging at him. Unease rattled him, after all day of dealing with the noises and the monsters, he wasn't used to it being this quiet. Or being this alone.

He avoided the images of the furry bastards dragging her to their den. His heart frantically pounded his rib cage. His vision went hazy with tears. Every dogman and human body poked, every puddle disturbed, every rock turned over. There had to be some sign of where she went…or was taken.

"Pull it together, man." Winston's hollow voice didn't exactly give him the confidence he'd hoped it would. Clearing his throat, he tried again. "If they took her, where would they have taken her? If she ran off, where would she have gone?"

Years of hunting them and coming up empty-handed came rushing back to him. His heart sank and he hung his head. He let down Jenn and now he was going to let down Lydia. Should he pack up and leave town? There was no way he'd be able to find her before they killed her. Winston kicked one of the dead dogmen. What did it matter that he killed them if he had nothing left? He stared at the gutter, the wet leaves, the urine, the bits of flesh. Laying there and dying seemed like a good idea. Then at least he could join Jenn and Lydia.

"Jenn, I think your silly old man fucked up. I think I got Lydia killed and I have no idea what to do." Winston's body tremored. "I don't know if I can find her. I really wish I had your help right now."

Talking to her made him think about her bench. In a million years he couldn't have predicted his day would have gone like this. What would have happened if he hadn't gone to tell her he was going to stop hunting the bastards? Bill wouldn't have been torn to shreds, at least, not then. Probably at some other point, though. Winston froze when it dawned on him where he had to go.

It was obvious and he should have known.

The scene of Jenn's death.

Winston released a deep sigh. That first dogman had come charging out of the woods behind her bench. And ten years ago, when he'd encountered the evil bastard that'd ruined his life, it'd been in that forest. Where else would they have taken Lydia, if they'd taken her, but there? It wasn't much. They could be anywhere in the forest. Would he be wasting Lydia's time if he checked? What if they weren't there? Could he face that patch of woods, with all the people who'd died heavy on his heart, with Lydia missing? Could he deal with more monsters?

For Lydia, he had to try.

Winston wished he could figure out how to get Lydia's speaker working. He stood in the center of the armory fiddling with the contraption. Building death-dealing weapons out of children's squirt guns was easy compared to hooking up a Bluetooth to a speaker. Not that he had time to deal with it, he was just looking for a distraction from what was coming. And loading up on a shitload of chocolate and weapons seemed like a good time for a montage.

"Focus, old man." He downed a few more painkillers and went to work.

They had cleared out most of his chocolate reserves for their first run. There was a strong chance this would be a suicide mission. But if he could get to her and distract the monsters long enough for her to escape it'd be okay. He scraped what he could get out of bowls, any spillage on tables, and the floor. He filled two glass bottles with a mixture of chocolate and gas for his snowblower. Half completed guns, untested things of tubes and nozzles, and a few stock Super Soakers were loaded up. It had to work. It had to be enough.

Depression clung to him. He stared at his messy hands. He felt old.

Jenn came to mind, and he shuffled over to her picture on the wall. His chocolate-covered fingerprint marring her face. Lydia's voice came next. *You're covered in chocolate; they can't stand it.* "Lydia, you're a fucking genius."

Winston slapped his hands into the melted chocolate on the table. He laughed and jumped into a puddle onto the floor like a kid after a rainstorm. Globs of goo splattered everywhere. He rushed out and headed for a boiler. A skin of hardening cocoa at the bottom snapped under his touch. He poked the thin layer of chocolatey goop and spread it on his face in lines. Next, he ripped the bloody sleeves off his shirt. Using his fingers, he painted tiger stripes across his skin, dark blood and chocolate mixing, until he became a candy-coated warrior.

"Those fuckers might take a bite out of me, but it'll be the last bite they take."

The war paint made his body sticky, and the sweet scent overwhelmed him. He stomped out of the shop, a gun in each hand, his mouth in a scowl. Dead monsters, chocolaty vomit, and blood marked the battlefield. His half-empty backpack thudded against his back as he dodged the bodies. Two belts around his waist held the last of his smaller squirt guns. In a pocket he had a butcher knife coated in dried chocolate. Dull pain wracked his body. The bastards wouldn't know what hit them.

He passed the town square and the corpses of dogmen lessened. Human remains plastered the street.

He paused at Stu's Hardware. *How different would it be if I didn't meet them here?* Despite not really liking them, they didn't deserve to die. Lowering his head, he whispered all their names. It would have been a nice moment if it wasn't for the stinky dogmen shit dotting the ground.

"God, that's fucking horrible."

Piles of poo were scattered all around the street. A semi straight line of dookie led south out of town. Winston followed the path with his eye, unable to believe how much waste the monsters could make. The ozone layer had to be burning.

"Oh fuck, that's perfect!"

The idea hit him as much as the stench. He cackled and, in a shambling gait, followed the trail. This brown brick road should lead him right to Lydia.

CHAPTER
TWENTY-FIVE

FOUR DOGMEN TUCKED tail and ran to the edge of town. Lydia followed.

These hairy bastards were the last ones she needed to kill before she was confident North Leeland was safe. They'd escaped her whirlwind of death after she had exploded out of the dogpile. Rage fueled her vision. She didn't slow down, avoid stepping on dogman bodies, blood puddles, or dog poo. Her shoes and pants were disgusting, she didn't care. The monsters were all that mattered. They'd taken everything from her, and she wasn't going to let them get away.

Something nagged at her as she passed the town square. The kind of feeling that would keep bugging her. Was she missing something? A quick mental scan told her she was missing her friends. Missing having a normal day. Maybe the BBQ. Missing at least another gallon or two of chocolate. Probably missing too much blood. Lydia glanced at the torn-up grass in the square, remembering lounging on a blanket reading a book or hanging out with the group for community movie night. She kept stalking the whining and panting beasts ahead of her. No, she knew she was missing all of those things. There was definitely something else. The clicking of claws grew fainter. She tore her gaze from the destroyed town center. The dogmen had increased the distance from her. Determination pushed out the worry, whatever she was thinking about would come back to her.

The hunted and hunter eventually reached the gas station and the barricade blocking the road. The dogmen scrambled over the fallen tree. Lydia shook her head at the monsters' awkward flailing limbs. They definitely weren't the brightest bulbs of the bunch. Though, they had endurance for days. She picked up her pace and aimed for the obvious easier path around the blockage. If only it would have been this easy to escape this morning. Then none of them would be dead. They could have gotten help. Once the beasts hit the grassy area between forest and road, they hustled toward the woods. She pushed herself to catch up when she came upon a forgotten brown truck.

Shock rippled through her, the thing she'd forgotten rushing to the forefront of her mind.

"Winston!"

She couldn't believe she'd left him behind. How could she have been so stupid? It would have taken two seconds to stop and check for her boss. Instead, she'd snapped and ran off, leaving him to die. Her heart sank. Maybe if she went back, she could save him. It might mean the monsters survived, but that would be fine. Saving Winston would have been one good thing she'd done today.

On the other hand, if the dogmen disappear, then who knows what other carnage they could cause. Lydia paced next to Bill's truck. The weight of the squirt-thrower felt good on her back, the handle of the gun a reassurance of what she'd been able to do. She gripped it tighter. Winston had made these to wipe the monsters off the face of the Earth. If he was dead, he had at least died doing what he wanted to do.

Gritting her teeth she turned her back on the town. Her friends might have argued with her plan at first, but they weren't here. All because of those hairy bastards. She imagined

Winston giving her guff if she went back for him instead of taking this opportunity to rid the world of these hairy fuckers. In the end it didn't matter what any of them thought, they were dead. She couldn't go back and save them. All she could do is stop it from happening to anyone else.

Wiping away the tears, Lydia dropped the squirt-thrower to the ground. She dug in her pockets and found a mini squirt gun and two bars of chocolate. A smirk crossed her face at the pressure nozzle added to the barrel's muzzle and the two rubber tubes full of chocolate. She appreciated the heft of the trigger's new mechanics that gave it an easy-to-squeeze trigger. Winston really was a mad genius. She glared at the edge of the woods. The perfect one-liner came to her, and she cackled. Somewhere in there was a group of dogmen. Soon, there'd be a group of dead dogmen.

In the dark, all the trees looked the same. Haphazard rows of gray, dark brown, and bluish trunks mocked her with the possible directions she could go. Lydia had no experience with hiking or tracking, besides watching that Bear Grylls show, but that only taught her about surviving on urine and talking to a camera crew, both of which she didn't want to do. At first it was easy, just follow the trail of dogshit. Then the poo markers became random drops with no discernable route to follow. Her resolve pushed her to keep going straight, though her tired body and sore muscles questioned if it was smart following poop. There was definitely some sort of metaphor there, she just couldn't come up with one. She walked, feeling more and more like she was going in circles.

After an indeterminant amount of time and passing a tree she was positive she'd passed once before, her ears perked up. Was she really hearing a howl or was she imagining the sound? She slowed and cocked her head. A moment later, the mournful cry came again. No way she was making it up. It had to be real. Excitement rippled through her. She focused and guessed it came from somewhere ahead of her.

The yodel-like sound didn't scare her as much as it did this morning. Could this be from the group she'd been following? Why weren't the others howling, too? Unless this was a different dogman. A fire burned in her gut. She squeezed the mini-squirter until her hand hurt. She'd wanted to believe the whole dogman species had converged on North Leeland, that they'd murdered them all. Besides the four she was following, of course. Those four would be dead soon. The possibility that there were more of these bastards pissed her off.

Whoa, you're starting to sound like Winston. Was this the way he felt for ten years? An impossible anger and drive to destroy something that took everything from you. It gave her a pause. Her heart broke at the idea he had to deal with these feelings all by himself. A slight worry crept over her that she could be like him if she wasn't careful. She was going to murder these last dogmen, there was no doubt, but she wasn't going to end up like Winston. She wasn't going to be the sad, crazy, person yelling about monsters in the woods, buying up squirt guns. No, if anything, this has shown her she needs to make sure she had the best life and not let something like this consume her.

As she dreamed about her new future, a black and brown dogman with a pointy snout and triangular ears much too big for its head pranced past her a few rows over. *Well, shit. Maybe my hearing was a little off.* Lydia blew out her nose, crouched and followed closely behind. The beast seemed to be heading towards an orange glow she hadn't noticed before. Much like its smaller, domesticated brethren, it didn't move in a straight line. No, it stopped to smell trees, chase its tail, roll around on its back in piles of leaves.

At first, she snuck from tree to tree, kept quiet, watched for possible attacks, but eventually she got bored. She didn't waste energy hiding as she kept her distance.

The longer she trailed the monster, the more she hoped it wasn't just on a stroll, that it was actually leading her to the others. The possibility that it had just left the group crossed her mind. She should kill this one and then retrace its steps to see if she'd passed them at some point. Though, the more she stared at the glow, the more it intrigued her. It could be a parking lot or a ranger station. Maybe there were people here. There was no way dogmen could string up lights. Why was it going to the light then? Was this one going to join its friends? Or did it sense humans and wanted a snack? She'd end this one, check the glow, then go back to exploring the woods. With the plan formed, she slunk up on the dogman as quiet as a ninja, the bar of chocolate in her hand. It continued its wandering and exploring without any signs it knew death followed.

The musky odor of wet fur, shit, and burnt meat, caused her to slow down a few yards from striking distance. *When did they learn how to cook?* The monster cocked its head, let out a low whine, scratched its snout, and bounded toward the light.

"Oh shit," she said, as she ducked behind a bush.

A sodium light attached to a telephone pole cast an orange glow on a clearing amongst the woods. Broken picnic tables were scattered near the edge of the space. However, she was more interested in the pièce de résistance: half a dozen dogmen chomping away at the remains of a smoked pig. *Well, that explains the BBQ smell.* Though she had no explanation for how or why the monsters had a smoked pig. The beast she was stalking ran up to a golden-haired friend and began sniffing its butt.

Lydia sunk down amongst the leaves. This *had* to be the last of them. If she could sneak up to them while they were distracted, she could probably take out two or three before they noticed. Then it'd be a fight. She wanted to believe she could win. The exhaustion, limited supply of chocolate, and litany of aches and pains had a different opinion. Sweat and cocoa cooled on her skin. It was one thing to be raging for violence and retribution, and another to actually do what you fantasized.

The dogmen continued digging into the pork. Lydia held the chocolate and judged the distance between her and the meat. Earlier she had perfect aim with tossing chocolate, could she do it a second time? It'd be way easier if she could deliver the poison and just sit back and relax. She tossed it up in the air and caught it a few times to get a feel for its weight. Mental calculations for the perfect arc raced through her head. There was no going back, no second thoughts. This had to be the last of the dogmen, and she was going to wipe them off the face of the earth.

Lydia shifted amongst the dead leaves until she had the right spot. Enough cover to be hidden, but a clear view of the pig carcass, and no branches to disrupt her throw. *Please let my chocolate fly true. Let the pig be warm enough to melt the chocolate. Let the dogmen eat the chocolate and die a horrible choking death on this gross ass chocolate. Let this be the last time I ever have to mess with this nasty-ass stuff. Amen.* With that she wound her arm back. As she started the process of performing the glorious throw, a flaming glass bottle flew the branches near her and completely disrupted her concentration. It landed with a thud in the center of the clearing, the fire sputtering out. Somewhere behind her someone cursed as the dogmen perked up, looked at the bottle, then growled in Lydia's direction.

"Well, fuck." Lydia and the mystery person said at the same time.

CHAPTER
TWENTY-SIX

AT THE EDGE OF TOWN, he came across the fallen trees that'd trapped North Leeland. Gary's truck stuck out of the barricade like a smashed metal arrow. *How has it only been a day?* A chill breeze rolled in from Lake Michigan, a darkening sky hung overhead. The quiet road slithered out of view. There were no headlights, sirens, or lines of people coming to save them from the massacre. Who really cared about a small town when it wasn't convenient? Winston snarled, he didn't need them, just Lydia. He tightened his grip on the guns and followed the piles of shit leading him to Jenn's bench and the woods hiding said monsters.

The forest loomed in front of him, a scary tangled wall going on forever. years ago, the government took control, labeling the place a national forest. Some hiking trails cut through the trees, but most of it was ancient and untouched. Dog poo created a dotted line to a break amongst the gray and brown trunks. Winston paused at the edge and wondered if he was stepping back in time. It was the kind of place found in a German fairytale. Some deep instinct told him witches, woodsmen, and emaciated insane children hid in there. *They better steer clear of me.*

The deeper into the woods, the less of the failing light snuck through amongst the branches and leaves, the delightful aroma of dogman shit his only guide. In the dark, he only had a vague idea where he'd camped with Jenn. Shadows in the forest played tricks on him, making it more of a wish. Which made him laugh. *Wish in one hand and shit in the other.*

Winston stopped walking. The monsters and Lydia could be anywhere. He listened. Silence. Not even a chirp from a squirrel or the crunch of leaves under a paw. His skin tightened around his scalp.

After a minute of hearing the thump of his heart, he picked up quiet crunching, slurping, and snorting. Winston cocked his head. A faint whiff of BBQ floated under the heady stank of dogman poo. Off to his right he spotted an orange glow peeking out from between the trees.

The urge to create a plan haunted him as he crept with a limp and stash of weapons. How to approach the dogmen, what to do when he got there, how many are there? Thoughts bombarded him and at first, he attempted to pick out what would work. He shook his head until the ideas fell into a deep well in his mind. Why did he need a plan now? The day had proven plans were pointless when it came to monsters.

Winston's muscles tightened at the sight of dogmen in the clearing, chomping down on a body. The whole world dropped out from under him. He was transported back to the moments after Jenn was attacked by the dogman. *No.* If it wasn't for his limp leg, if he hadn't wasted time in the fudge shop, he could have stopped this from happening. Now the bastards were having her for a snack. He stumbled back into the shadows. His mind blanked. The crackle of leaves, the crunching of bones, and the lapping of blood was all he knew.

Rage boiled and bubbled in his guts. These hairy sons of bitches were not taking anyone else. Winston's muscles tensed, energy coursing through him. They were going to face a whole lot of hell. He was ready to die and take all of them with him.

And the best way to do that was with all the chocolate he had. He dug into his pack and pulled out one of the altered Molotov Cocktails. Melted cocoa and gasoline sloshed around inside. He stuffed one of his torn shirt sleeves into the bottle. The chaos and panic he hoped it would cause put a smile on his face.

"Here's to saying fuck it and seeing what happens."

Pulling his lighter out of his pocket, Winston lit the fuse and hurled the homemade chocolate explosive into the clearing. The bottle flew in a wonderful arc. The torn shirt sleeve sticking out dripped flames along its path. It was like waiting for Max Booth III's birthday fireworks. He held the other bottle, ready for round two. He imagined the spraying of chocolate, the confusion of the dogmen reacting to the explosion, the shattered glass coated in their kryptonite shredding the monsters' skin. It'd be glorious. Then it hit an empty patch of dirt near a group of beasts.

The flame sputtered out and nothing happened.

"Well, fuck," Winston said.

The dogmen paused midmeal to glare in the direction the bottle came from. They growled in what could only be inter-preted as "what the fuck? We're eating here!" A skinny dogman with a sharp pointed snout and ridiculously tall ears went to the bottle and poked it with its foot. The group glanced at each other then back in Winston's direction when nothing happened. A golden-haired dogman rapidly barked at its friends and pointed back and forth between them and the woods.

Winston didn't need to understand their language to get the gist of what was being conveyed: "Hey, I think someone might be here."

The clearing didn't completely erupt into the chaos he'd hoped for. Two monsters lowered their ears and growled at the golden-haired one, another took a few steps forward then laid down and whined, and one barked and pointed back at the de facto leader. This led to them yapping and bristling, slapping chests, and shaking fists.

If there was ever an opportunity to take advantage of, he

knew it was this. He charged into the area with his guns squirting. The monsters' argument was forgotten as they joined forces to meet him in the middle, with hackles raised and foam coating their lips. He had no time, nor mental fortitude to see Lydia's chewed upon body, the dogmen were on him faster than he expected. Direct hits to their open maws sent them spiraling. He jumped over a dying, hairy body. Brown liquidy throw-up coated grass, clung to fur, and sunk into the dirt. Unlike the rage he'd felt before, this time he felt in control. No wasted chocolate, no blind madness making him reckless, every kill encouraging him, filling his body with energy. He'd have these bastards dead in no time.

With this simple counting-your-eggs-before-they-hatch thought, he had to pay the price. The price? An empty tank right when a black-and-white spotted dogman loomed near him.

"Shit."

The monster knocked him into the air with one furry arm. Winston landed with a thunk onto his back, the tank digging into his spine, stars dancing in his vision. He fought through the pain as the dalmatian-like beast stalked closer. It stopped in its tracks above his prone body, pawed at its snout, and stumbled back. *Dang, that's right, I'm covered in chocolate!* Terrible laughter burst out of him, straining his hurt ribs, while he struggled to sit and rip the pack off. He yanked out one of the handheld guns. Steadying his trembling arm, he squeezed the trigger and sent a short stream of brown liquid up the dogman's nose.

Winston tempted fate by searching for Lydia's body. He couldn't help himself, he had to see her one last time. Confusion crossed his mind when he saw her. Unless the bastards had somehow eaten all of her clothes and hair, something wasn't right. He didn't have time to ponder this as the air was knocked out of him.

Holding his stomach, he whipped around and faced a buff dogman standing above him. The springy-haired monster had its leg pulled back for another kick. He couldn't help being confused by this new form of attack as the paw and its sharp claws connected with his side. Stars and darkness clouded his vision. It took everything in him to keep from passing out. Lydia's face floated before him. He couldn't be finished, not yet, he had to know if that body was her. The beast wound up for another kick, balancing on one leg. Winston almost felt bad when he grabbed the supporting leg and twisted. The dogman tumbled to the ground with a yelp. Snagging the chocolate-coated knife at his side, Winston plunged the blade in and out of the monster, using the leverage of each stab to pull himself up the bastard's body. Blood and chocolate oozed out of fresh wounds, its whining getting higher with each plunge of the knife until Winston finally sliced its hairy throat.

Attempting to jump to his feet, Winston found only half his body complied and he sorta sat there. The world became liquid before his eye, his muscles flashed their old man warning, his bones crunched and cracked. The day caught up to him and demanded its price. He punched and rubbed his legs, his heart jackhammering against his ribcage, cold sweat streaked his clammy skin. *Not now.*

A tree trunk of a furry paw slammed down in front of him. Black claws tipped each toe, wiry black hairs bristled around a shapely calf. Winston's focus trailed up the creature's buff body until he stared into the murderous eyes of the biggest dogman he had ever faced. Those eyes! Never in the last ten years had he forgotten them. He saw Jenn's mangled body reflected in their glow. How could it be here now? Panic, anger, regret, and sadness burned through his mind. Yet, his body left him help-less, forcing him to sit and face the thing that ruined his life.

Frustrated tears streaked his cheeks as the beast grabbed him by the scruff of his neck and yanked him up in the air like he was a puppy. His legs dangled uselessly. Without waiting for any scare tactics from the monster, Winston punched the bastard's head. His knuckles cracked and jagged shards of pain shot up his forearm. The dogman growled, its rotten meat breath washing over his face, and it tossed him over its shoulder like he was a floppy chew toy.

Darkness overtook him when he landed. Pain became the only thing he knew. He swore he heard Jenn or Lydia calling to him. He followed their voice, drifting away from his body.

Hey, get up.

"I think I'm done for."

Bullshit. I've never seen you give up.

"This is a little different than those stupid Sudoku puzzles."

I don't think so. (Sudoku? What the fuck are you talking about?) Remember how you never stopped working on the plumbing under the sink, even though you flooded the basement? (Dude, you gotta get up.) Or that time you wanted to win that truck, so you stood next to it for two full days?

"Ha, yeah. I don't think I've ever shit my pants like that before."

He lost track of where he was floating. The world faded into a foggy mist. "It's time I joined you. I think I figured out what you meant by being free, just took me some time. But I'm good now."

TWENTY-SEVEN

LYDIA ONLY CONSIDERED the origin of the dud mystery bottle for a moment before Winston burst onto the scene. Her heart skipped a beat. He was alive. And apparently pissed off, diving right into the group of dogmen without hesitation. Relief flushed her system. She slipped out of her hiding spot, figuring out the best way to hug him, let him know she was here, and join the battle at the same time. Rustling and short barks on the right side of the clearing stopped her. A gang of new dogmen, including a beefy nasty-looking motherfucker in the lead, stalked into the opening and zeroed in on her boss. She cracked her neck, decided there'd be time later for a celebratory reunion, and crept toward the newcomers.

As Lydia avoided branches and dead leaves, she told herself this had to be the last of the monsters. It was getting annoying thinking this so often. She couldn't help doing it, how were there so many of them? Before she could come up with an answer, her foot snagged a root. She caught herself midtrip and cursed herself for not paying attention to her path. How could she, when Winston was growling, the dogmen were growling, and the new monsters were doing their weird bark laughing? Refocusing on watching her steps, she was thankful the dogmen had stuck to the sidelines watching the fight. The more they were distracted, the better chance she had on sneaking up on them. Eventually these bastards were going to get bored and jump in, she had to stop them before it happened.

Lydia welcomed the lucky break, moments before stepping on a hard, slick object. Fuck. Her hands flew out, her legs did cartoonish kicks, and she stammered. Time stopped to allow her to really feel her embarrassment, to really wallow in the fact that she'd probably die in such a ridiculous fashion. Once it decided she had enough, it started back up and she regained her balance, but not much of her composure. How could she have let herself get distracted again? What the fuck did she step on? Did the dogmen notice her? There was no way they couldn't have, they were probably on their way right now. She readied herself to be face-to-face with one and checked.

Nothing but leaves and air. The bastards were still in their original spot, slapping each other on the back, pointing, and nodding along to the fight. Lydia fumed. Before she stomped over to kick their asses, she had an urge to tear at the thing that embarrassed her. Another bottle. Winston must have dropped it when he ran into the clearing. The aroma of gas and chocolate made her smile. *He always had a trick up his sleeves.* She took it with her and slunk to an ideal spot to give these dogmen a bad day.

As soon as she settled in and planned the perfect trajectory, the monsters growled, stomped their feet, and charged into the fracas. Winston had taken out their friends during her trek and the group didn't seem happy. *What the hell is going on with my luck today?* The nasty-looking dogman took the lead, yet all of its muscles didn't help much as the others passed it. There was no time to figure out why the first bottle didn't explode. If all of them got to Winston, he'd be overwhelmed. She lit the fabric sticking out of the opening, aimed for a scruffy dogman near the end of the pack, and chucked the incendiary device.

Glass, fire, and chocolate exploded on the dogman. Any

monsters near it were shredded and poisoned from the splash back. The beasts whined and dropped, vomiting and kicking in their death throes. Lydia pumped her fist. Then her body drooped, and she sighed as the others continued running, not even glancing back at their dying friends. A springy-haired dogman reached Winston first and kicked him. Well, she at least took a few out. She steeled herself and ran in to cut off any of the stragglers.

The ensuing battle was glorious. Lydia used the skills she'd learned throughout the day to decimate the remaining dogmen. Winston was her goal, and no monster was going to get in her way. Chocolate was squirted. Vomit was vomited. Urine was urinated. Dogmen crumpled. The clearing became a killing ground. Yet, she couldn't quite reach her boss.

The dogman lifted Winston and tossed him across the area with a snarl. He landed in a painful-looking heap. It strutted towards his limp body like a pro wrestler going in for their finishing move. Lydia ran at the beast, her gun sputtering out the last bit of its chocolate. If she could just get close enough, she could jam it down the beast's throat. Yet, when she got in striking range, it backhanded her and sent her sprawling. She landed with a thud and splashed into a puddle of chocolate vomit.

Winston lifted his head for a moment before plopping back down. He grumbled and whispered something Lydia could barely make out.

"What are you talking about? You have to get up!"

Seconds ticked by and it seemed like this was it, she was going to lose him. Again. Lydia searched for something she could throw or shoot. She had to stop the monster, had to save her friend. There was an orange reflection on her right. A knife covered in gore and chocolate. *Jackpot.* She scooped up the weapon and yelled as the monster got down on all fours.

"I'll kill you, you son of a bitch!"

CHAPTER
TWENTY-EIGHT

THE VOICE OF A WARRIOR, the voice of a friend, guided him back to the world.

Winston slammed back into his body. Was he imagining Lydia's voice? Maybe that body wasn't hers, maybe she had escaped at some point. He didn't have much capacity to put together any more thoughts. Pain threaded through him to the point he couldn't imagine what it felt like to not be in pain. Instead of fighting it, he fed off the damage. His one eye flickered open, zeroing in on the mass of bloodthirsty fur and teeth above him.

The wiry mega dogman towered over Winston and put its hands on its hips. The fur on its back flared up in a ridge. Molten fire burned in its black eyes. It pulled back its lips in triumph, revealing finger-length fangs.

I'm not done yet.

Concentrating and fighting back tears, he attempted to gain control over his arms. *If I can just grab my knife.* When his hand slapped his side, he found nothing. Fuck. Throughout the day he was positive he'd win. He just had to keep going, keep trying. He couldn't lose. Today had proven he was right; he could handle whatever it threw at him. Yet, as the dogman savored and gloated over its victory, he realized life didn't care about you. Things happen and there's nothing you can do.

The giant dogman dropped to all fours. It nudged him with its nose. Sniffed a few times. Saliva leaked out of its mouth and pooled on the ground as it opened its jaws. Teeth punctured bicep, he couldn't feel it, only witnessed the blood seeping out around the fangs. He hoped it choked on him, or he gave it indigestion, and it got really sick.

Movement and crunching dirt came from the right and sneaked into the spaces of his brain that weren't focused on being eaten.

Lydia?

She crept toward the monster, with his chocolate coated knife in her hand. A spark pulsed through him. It didn't matter that this bastard dogman was chomping down on his arm, warmth filled his heart. Lydia was alive! He hadn't imagined her voice. She survived and appeared to be ready to kick some ass. This was a world he wanted to live in, one where the dogmen were dead, Lydia was here, and he could do what Jenn always wanted him to do. Scratch all that nonsense about life not caring about you, and there's nothing you can do. Lydia was fucking doing something. He put all of his energy into gaining control over his body. He wanted to see his friend kill this beast.

The beast whined and stopped mid-bite. It released his limb, a string of blood and drool hanging between dogman and human. Twitching, the monster scooted away from Winston. A bleeding Lydia hung from the butcher knife plunged into the beast.

"Let him go, you son of a bitch!" She winked at Winston and jerked the knife.

The dogman shook Lydia off its body. She landed with an oof. The monster awkwardly reached for the knife in the middle of its back, missing it by a mile. With a gagging cough, the dogman's attempt at standing ended with it stumbling onto the dirt.

There's still chocolate on the blade! Winston laughed, blood and phlegm sputtering out of his mouth. Everything throbbed with pain. He groaned as he struggled to his elbows, excited he could finally move, that he wasn't dead. Hell, he was even excited for the pain tomorrow. Nausea played havoc with his head. He focused on Lydia as she swayed toward him. He motioned for her to stop. Next to him was the final squirt gun, he nudged it to her and winked before collapsing.

Shuffling footsteps scraped the ground. Gross hacking noises came from his right. The dogman's body creaked. Lydia coughed and spit, the loogie smacking dirt with a plop. Plastic squeaked. The monster responded with a guttural mournful howl. Winston imagined it was a pithy one-liner.

"Game over," Lydia said, as pressurized chocolate hissed through a tube.

Winston opened his eyelid enough to see the dogman, the last dogman in the clearing, choke on chocolate. Lydia dropped the gun and fell next to Winston.

"We did it. They're gone."

TWENTY-NINE

THE LAKE MICHIGAN breeze welcomed them out of the forest. Orange, red, and violet light painted the sky. Waves gently crashed against the shore. A picture-perfect scene anyone would appreciate at a moment like this. As long as they ignored the random landmines of dogman shit. The hint of smoke from burning buildings. The eerie silence coming from a vacation town. Yet, all Lydia and Winston could focus on was a lonely bench facing the water.

They stumbled and limped across the grass. Blood, chocolate, and sweat coated their bodies. Muscles ached. Wounds leaked. Thoughts were hazy. Neither of them spoke on their trek. There was no discussion on where they were heading, they both knew the destination. Lydia helped Winston along, allowing him to use her as a crutch. She didn't mind holding him up but couldn't wait to sit down. They crossed the road as the sun was barely peaking over the horizon, and they plopped onto the bench.

"Fuck, is it over?" Lydia asked.

Winston's eye was closed, his chin resting on his barely rising chest, his hands on his lap. She watched him, praying he wasn't on his last breath. He couldn't be, not now. Just when she was about to poke him he spoke up. "I think it is. You did great kid."

Lydia studied the waves, mesmerized by how nature kept going no matter what else was happening. Winston opened his eye and glanced up at the sky, sighing and then groaning.

"So, what are you going to do now?" Winston winced as he faced her.

"What do you mean?"

"I mean, I'm probably going to sit here for a while, maybe finish bleeding out and die, and finally be with Jenn."

"You're not going to die. You're a tough son of a bitch." Lydia wiped her face. "We're going to get you some help."

His chuckle morphed into a coughing fit, flecks of blood mixing with the chocolate stains on his shirt. "That's cute. But seriously—"

"No, shut up and listen. You're going to live. We're going to get in a car, get you to a hospital, and get help for this fucking town."

Winston grinned, enjoying this version of Lydia. He always had a theory she was in there just waiting to come out.

"After that, you and are going to open the shop. But it's not going to be a fudge shop. I think I've had enough of it for one lifetime."

"Maybe it should be a pet store?"

THE END

ACKNOWLEDGMENTS

So, I have a confession. I absolutely adore the *John Wick* movies; they are on the list of my comfort watches(though I do fast forward through the dog killing scene). Give me ridiculous over-the-top action and I'm a happy boy. Give me a hero that can somehow survive so much blood loss, getting hit by cars, stabbed and beaten, and I want more.

This one isn't really a confession, because it's fucking rad, but I love *The Warriors*. A gang fighting a bunch of other crazy gangs through New York to get to their home turf of Coney Island? Uh, yes please.

Here's the real confession. I have a shirt designed by the great Rob Schrab (*Community, Rick & Morty, The Sarah Silverman Project, Channel 101*) that features a fake movie cover for *Willy Wonka Werewolf Hunter*. I wanted this movie to exist so badly. It's just such an obvious idea that hasn't really been explored…

So, I stole the idea, tossed in some of the action I love, and just a bit of humor, mixed it all up, and got this. Thank you for tasting and enjoying it!

*Also, you should definitely look up chocolate cheese. Oh, and listen to Direct Hit!'s Werewolf Shame (or the Mixtapes' version, which I like more), it's a great song and I listened to it a lot while writing this.

There's a lot of people I want to thank that helped me with the insanity that you just read. Thank you to Ryan Bradley for being an early reader! Ruth Anna Evans for the absolutely killer cover, definitely check her out for your covers! Carson Winter for the layout and design! Betty Rocksteady for the Sleight of Hand logo!

Special thanks to Max Booth III for editing. Your advice lifted this ridiculous adventure into something super cool and much closer to the story in my head. You helped me become a better writer with your suggestions and comments. And hey, your challenge was accepted and you're in the book! Also, if anyone wants it, Lydia's Bowels is available for your band name.

Kirsten Noelle Craig, you are the most amazing, lovely, caring, sweet, brilliant person in the world. I can't thank you enough for your help with reading this, with suggestions on how to release this thing, helping with the back cover, for supporting and encouraging me, for listening, for being there, for being you. I will forever be in your debt and there for you. For all time.

My Staring Into the Abyss gang. Richard Gerlach and Villimey Mist, you two are super rad and it's been amazing how long we've been rambling about books and movies.

My gremlins, Finley and Hazel. Hopefully it's not too embarrassing having a dad that wrote about chocolate vomit and following a trail of dog poo. I'm so proud of you both.

Finally, Rob Schrab for inspiring me with your T-shirt. One day I'd love for you to read this. If anyone reading this has some random connection to him, let me know!

Hey, you're still reading this, that's great! Here's a list of people you all should be reading. Look them up, buy their books, tell them they are awesome! Carson Winter, Laurel Hightower, Alex Ebenstein, Maria Dong, Tamika Thompson, Michael Dixon, Justin Lutz, Joe Koch, Ryan Bradley, Kyle Winkler, Jonathan

Raab, Zin E Rocklyn, Matthew Mitchell, Patrick Barb, Kirsten Noelle Craig, Matt Forgit, Laura Bolger, Christopher Hawkins, Sam Richard, Danger Slater, Josh Rountree, Valentina Rojas, Michael Bettendorf, Charlene Elsby, Valkyrie Loughcrewe.

ABOUT THE AUTHOR

Matt Brandenburg is a horror writer living next to a moldy pumpkin patch in Kalamazoo, Michigan. He is the author of ... *And Out Come the Toys*. You can find some of his short stories in 34 Orchard, No Lives Left, Novus Monstrum, and Tales to Terrify. He is also a cohost on the podcast Staring into the Abyss. When he's not writing cartoonish horror, he is usually listening to horror movie scores, watching goofy movies, or playing with Lego. Find him on Bluesky and his website matt-brandenburg.com

ALSO BY MATT BRANDENBURG

...And Out Come the Toys